OSAUR

GUY BASS
ILLUSTRATED BY LEE ROBINSON

To the comics, cartoons and action figures of my childhood.
And to my wife, Ruth...
...who puts up with the comics, cartoons and action figures of my adulthood.
– Guy Bass

Thanks, Mum!
– Lee Robinson

stripes

When top *spy*-entists put the mind of super-spy Agent Gambit inside the body of a dinosaur, they created the first ever **Super Secret Agent Dinosaur**. Together with his daughter, Amber, this prehistoric hero protects the world from villainy.

His codename:

FROM A LAND BEFORE TIME COMES A HERO FOR TODAY...

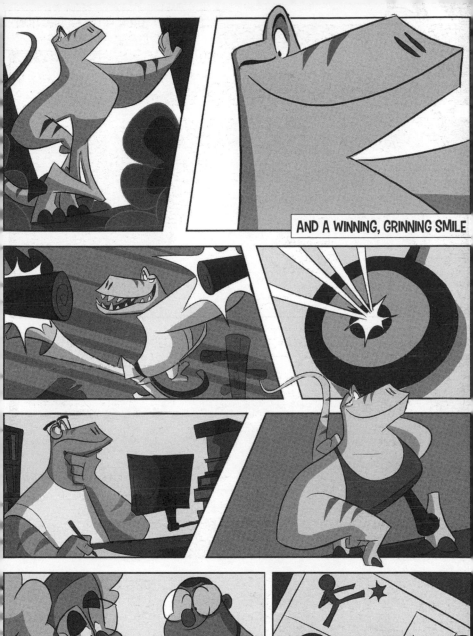

AND A WINNING, GRINNING SMILE

HE'S THE DARING DAPPER DINO WITH THE PREHISTORIC STYLE!

HE'S THE SCALED 'N' TAILED AGENT WHO IS CERTAIN TO SURPRISE

BUT HE STILL LOOKS LIKE A DINOSAUR, WHATEVER HIS DISGUISE

SPYNOSAUR!

1.
THE DOUBLE

⊕ **No.13 DIGGLE DRIVE,
THE VILLAGE OF LITTLE WALLOP**

BA-DEEP!
BA-DEEP!
BA-DEEP!

Amber woke with a start. She sat up in bed and glanced over to her Super Secret Spy Watch™, which beeped incessantly.

"The signal!" she whispered. In twenty-seven seconds she was dressed and racing downstairs.

"Morning, Amber" said her mum, as Amber hurried past her on the stairs. "What do you want for breakfast?"

"Toast, please!" Amber replied. She waited for her mum to disappear into the kitchen before tiptoeing to the front-room window and sliding it open. Hiding in the bushes under the window was a very short, old man with a craggy face and a permanent scowl.

He was Amber's exact height, wore a tracksuit identical to hers, and atop his head sat a wig just like Amber's bob of red hair.

"Sergei does not like the toast," grunted Sergei in a thick, deep growl. "Sergei likes Coco Pops."

"Sorry, Sergei, I forgot," said Amber with a wink. She clambered out of the window as Sergei clambered in. Once inside, Sergei adjusted his wig and brushed a leaf off his tracksuit, just as Amber's mum returned from the kitchen.

"Toast won't be a minute, Amber," she said, kissing Sergei on top of the head.

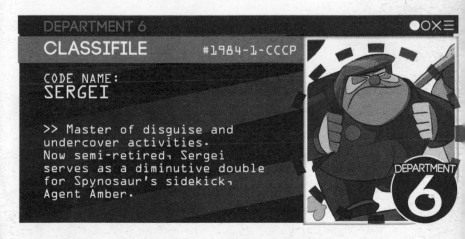

DEPARTMENT 6 ●○O✕☰

CLASSIFILE #1984-1-CCCP

CODE NAME:
SERGEI

>> Master of disguise and undercover activities.
Now semi-retired, Sergei serves as a diminutive double for Spynosaur's sidekick, Agent Amber.

DEPARTMENT
6

"Toast..." he grunted. "Thank you, mother of Amber. I mean, Mother."

"Well, you've got to keep your strength up – big day at school," added Amber's mum.

Sergei let out a long sigh. "School..." he grunted to himself. "Sergei is getting too old for this."

2.
THE MISSION

No.13 DIGGLE DRIVE, THE VILLAGE OF LITTLE WALLOP

While Amber's double reluctantly awaited his toast, the real Amber was already speeding down the road on her bicycle. She was just out of sight of her house when a familiar low hum filled the air. The postman cycling towards her waved at Amber, before watching her and her bike suddenly rise up into the air and disappear.

DIGGLE DRIVE

"Woohoo!" cried Amber, as she and her bike were swallowed up inside an almost-invisible aircraft by a powerful gravity beam. She emerged into a garage-sized docking bay and hopped off her bicycle.

DEPARTMENT 6   ●○O✕≡

CLASSIFILE   #1984-DZ-DB8

CODE NAME:
THE DINO-SOARER

>> Supersonic saurian-styled stealth jet. Specially adapted for pilots with tails. Equipped with invisibility mode, gravity beam, missile launchers, front and rear laser cannons and built-in Wi-Fi.

DEPARTMENT
6

"Hi, Dad! So what's the mission?" Amber asked, crossing the docking bay towards the Dino-soarer's cockpit.

"Saving the world, of course," said a low, clipped voice.

Standing before her was a dinosaur. The scaly, green *Deinonychus* measured a full nine feet from head to tail, with huge claws on his hands and feet, a long, broad head and a wide mouth filled with razor-sharp teeth. He wore a sleek spy-suit, with a silver pistol tucked into a shoulder holster.

Amber threw herself at the dinosaur and hugged him tightly.

"I missed you, too, poppet," he said, wrapping his deadly claws round her.

"Da-ad, I told you not to call me that," Amber groaned. "I'm a super secret agent..."

"Super secret agent in *training*," corrected her dad. "How's your mother?"

"OK, I s'pose," Amber replied with a shrug. "I don't see her much, what with all this spy stuff – Sergei spends more time with her than I do. Are you sure we can't just tell her the truth?"

"And admit we're spies? Out of the question," replied Spynosaur. "I'll always love your mother, but she can't keep a secret to save her life. Do you remember the time you asked her not to tell anyone that you accidentally flushed your pet gerbil down the toilet? It was all over the village by teatime! No, I'm afraid your mum believes that

I was a travelling peanut-butter salesman who died in a tragic kite-flying accident. We're spies, Amber — keeping secrets is what we do."

"I s'pose," Amber sighed.

"Good girl," said Spynosaur. "Now, have you been practising your **NINJA SKILLS**?"

"Every day!" replied Amber, kicking and punching at him furiously.

"Ah, the **HASTY PUFFERFISH OPEN SANDWICH DRAINPIPE ATTACK** — excellent work, poppet," said Spynosaur, casually deflecting her blows with his tail.

"*Please* stop calling me—" Amber began. But she was interrupted by a voice blaring out from the cockpit's control panel.

SPYNOSAUR! COME IN, SPYNOSAUR!

"The **DEPARTMENT 6** top-secret transmission channel!" Amber cried, as Spynosaur pressed a button on the Dino-soarer's control panel. A woman's face appeared on the cockpit viewscreen. She had a neatly cropped bob of greying hair and an impressive moustache.

"M11! Missing me already?" Spynosaur grinned, flashing his sharp teeth.

"Spynosaur, if it were up to me you'd be extinct," snarled M11. "As far as I'm concerned, your maverick methods and routine recklessness have no place in Department 6. You were more than enough trouble when you were human, but—"

"—*But* since I continue to save the world on a bi-weekly basis, you'll let me off," interrupted Spynosaur, giving Amber a wink.

"Blast it to smithereens, Spynosaur, just pay attention," M11 sighed. "A week ago, we began intercepting coded messages between high-ranking members of your favourite international crime syndicate."

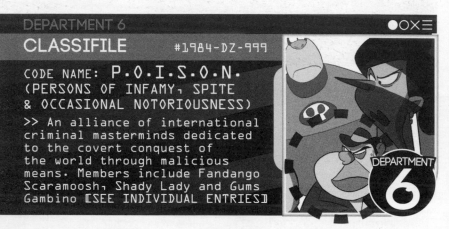

DEPARTMENT 6 ●○○✕≡

CLASSIFILE #1984-DZ-999

CODE NAME: P.O.I.S.O.N.
(PERSONS OF INFAMY, SPITE
& OCCASIONAL NOTORIOUSNESS)

>> An alliance of international criminal masterminds dedicated to the covert conquest of the world through malicious means. Members include Fandango Scaramoosh, Shady Lady and Gums Gambino [SEE INDIVIDUAL ENTRIES]

DEPARTMENT 6

"**P.O.I.S.O.N.**?" hissed Spynosaur. "What are those diabolical do-no-gooders up to now?"

"The P.O.I.S.O.N. bigwigs are planning a meeting to consider the recruitment of a new member," M11 continued. "None other than your former nemesis, Ergo Ego."

CLASSIFILE   #1984-DZ-015

NAME:
ERGO EGO PHD·OMG·LOL·

>> Criminal mastermind and
all-round bad egg-head· Creator
of the Mind Mining Machine, a
device that copies a person's
brainwaves and downloads them
to a pocket-sized "brain
box"· Subject is obsessed
with gaining the respect of
other criminal masterminds,
specifically the P·O·I·S·O·N·
high command·

DEPARTMENT 6

"Ego's alive?" Spynosaur growled, clenching his clawed fists. "I thought he was destroyed when you blew up his secret island lair in the Bermuda Triangle after he tied me to a space rocket and fired me into the moon!"

"And after I fought Ego for the brain box that contained your brainwaves," added Amber proudly.

"You did very well, poppet," her father noted, before returning to the screen. "Why didn't you tell me, M11? Why didn't you assign me the mission in the first place?"

"Because, blast it to smithereens, Spynosaur, I knew you'd make it personal!" snapped M11. "Making things personal is what reckless, rule-book-ignoring mavericks do!"

"Shooting someone into the moon *is* personal!" growled Amber.

"The point is, we have reason to believe Ego has created some sort of super-secret weapon, known only as the *McGuffin*," M11 continued. "He plans to hand the weapon over to P.O.I.S.O.N. in exchange for membership of their guild."

"He's been desperate to join that felonious faction for years," said Spynosaur. "Where is Ego now?"

"That's the problem — we've had your former partner secretly tracking Ego for weeks — but two days ago we lost all contact," M11 explained.

"Sounds like *Danger Monkey* needs me to save his tail again," said Spynosaur.

"Your mission is to locate Danger Monkey and secure the McGuffin," concluded M11. "Preferably without blowing up everything in sight."

"Never fear, M11, we'll find the Department's prized primate and this weapon of mass mischief – and put a stop to Ergo Ego for good measure," Spynosaur assured her. "*And* we'll be back for Amber's bedtime."

"Da-ad," groaned Amber.

3.
MISSING 'N' ACTION

 HIGH ABOVE THE MOUNTAINS
SOMEWHERE

The Dino-soarer had been in the air for more than an hour, speeding silently through the skies at supersonic speed. As Amber piloted the craft, Spynosaur sat beside her reviewing the mission briefing.

"Dad, we're coming up on Danger Monkey's last-known location," said Amber, checking the viewscreen.

"Good! So, we rescue Danger Monkey, find the McGuffin and slap Ego in chains," said Spynosaur, checking his pistol. "And all the while being cooler than a cucumber in the—"

"Snow!" gasped Amber, pressing her hands against the cockpit window as she peered out at a vast, snow-covered mountain range. After a moment, she glared at Spynosaur and saw a glint in his yellow eye. "Dad, don't even think about—"

"*Snow* puns at all – got it," he replied. He tapped at his Super Secret Spy Watch™ with a sharp claw. "Set the Dino-soarer to autopilot – it's time to brave the elements."

Spynosaur retrieved a puffer jacket from an overhead compartment and handed it to Amber.

By the time she'd donned her spy gear, Spynosaur was dressed from head to tail in a fur-collared cold-weather suit, complete with parachute.

"Where's my parachute?" asked Amber

Spynosaur scooped her up and held her to his chest. "Not until you're at least twelve," he said. He positioned himself in the middle of the docking bay and tapped his Super Secret Spy Watch™. "Now, let's get some fresh air, shall we?"

Amber heard a **CLUNK!** and a **WHIRRRR**... Then she felt her stomach lurch as the floor of the Dino-soarer slid open, dropping them into the air.

They plummeted downwards, freefalling towards the snow-covered mountains. Spynosaur stretched out his powerful tail to change direction.

"AAAAAH-*mazing*!" cried Amber as they fell.

Spynosaur pulled a cord on his harness and the parachute opened with a **FWUMPH!** A moment later they were floating slowly towards a carpet of low-lying clouds.

"Remember, a good spy sees everything, misses nothing and never repeats himself. And sees everything," said Spynosaur. "Let's play our game, shall we?"

"I spy with my little eye..." began Amber, glancing around. This was a game they'd played hundreds of times, but Amber rarely matched the keenness of her dad's uncanny *spy-sight*. "I spy with my little eye ... I spy with— Wait...! There! I see something!"

A pair of stone towers jutted out from beneath the cloud line. Atop a mountain, surrounded

by a small
army of tall
pine trees, was a
fort built from grey
stone.

"Well spotted, poppet.
Ergo Ego's hideout, no doubt,"
said Spynosaur, directing their
descent towards the fort. "Let's
see if we can't wrap this case
up before lunch. I have a sudden
hankering for live goats..."

"Eeeeeew! Da-ad, I'm a *vegetarian*,"
groaned Amber.

Spynosaur aimed for a high, arched window in
the tallest tower ... then he held Amber close and
detached his parachute. He stretched his body
out to its full length and crashed through the
window like a scaly spear.

With a rapid roll, Spynosaur was back on his feet and depositing Amber on the floor.

"Hope you don't mind us dropping in on you, Ego!" declared Spynosaur, drawing his pistol. "Now surrender, or— Oh, there's no one in here."

They found themselves in a large, dusty hall, strewn with shattered glass and upturned furniture. It was as if a tornado had swept through. At the far end of the room was a large portrait of Ergo Ego standing in a lake and holding a fishing rod.

"I spy with my little eye..." said Amber, her eyes darting around the room for clues. She ran her fingers along the leg of an upturned table, then gave them a tentative sniff.

"Ew, ew, ew!" she screamed. "Monkey poo!"

"I thought I smelled something," noted Spynosaur. He holstered his pistol and paced across the room, his toe claws **CLIK-CLAK**-ing on the floor. "Danger

Monkey was here all right, and it looks like he was in full *fling*. It must have been quite a tussle. Or perhaps..."

Spynosaur stopped dead in front of Ergo Ego's portrait. There was a large splat of monkey poo covering Ego's face.

"...Or perhaps he was trying to *tell* us something," added Spynosaur. He struck the wall with his tail, sending the painting crashing to the floor. Behind it, hidden in an alcove carved out of the wall, was a small silver attaché case, no bigger than two lunchboxes and locked with a thick brass padlock.

"The McGuffin!" gasped Amber excitedly, as Spynosaur pulled the case from its hiding place. "You found it!"

"That does seem like the sort of achingly impressive thing I'd do," said Spynosaur, inspecting the case. "But if this is the McGuffin, why would Ego leave it here unguarded? Unless— Wait."

"What is it?" whispered Amber.

"My super-spy senses are doing their super-spy thing," he said, making his way to the window. "Can you hear that? Sounds like ... something diabolical. Sounds like..."

"Like what?" said Amber. She followed her dad to the window and they peered up. The low clouds had parted to reveal blue sky and a bright, yellow-white sun.

Spynosaur squinted. There was something flying towards them at high speed.

"Like a dino-seeking missile!" Spynosaur cried. He scooped Amber up in one hand and the attaché case in the other. Then he leaped through the window on powerfully prehistoric legs ... just as the missile rushed over their heads and into the fort.

BOOM!

4.
ATTACK
OF THE
NINJA SNOWMEN

Spynosaur gripped Amber to his chest as the force of the explosion blew them through the air. Searing flames and rubble accompanied them as they fell, spinning and spiralling to the ground below. They crashed through a snow-covered pine tree, Spynosaur's dense, dinosaurian body snapping branch after branch until he finally landed in a mound of mercifully soft snow.

"AAH! And OW!" yelped Amber as Spynosaur got to his feet. He deposited his daughter on the ground and casually extinguished a small fire on his left arm.

"Well, I'd say our cover is well and truly *blown*,"

he noted, looking up at the flaming remains of the fort. Then he held up the attaché case to check it was intact.

"Who tried to blow us up? I'll ninja kick them to bits!" declared Amber. "But wait, where's Danger Mo—?"

WHI/////////////////////SH!

Amber didn't even see the blade spinning towards her head. With the unmatched reflexes of the world's first and only super-secret agent dinosaur, Spynosaur swung the attaché case in front of her face just in time. The blade embedded in the metal case with a **SHHUN K!**

"Talk about getting to the *point*," said Spynosaur, plucking the deadly blade from the case to get a closer look.

It was in the shape of a snowflake.

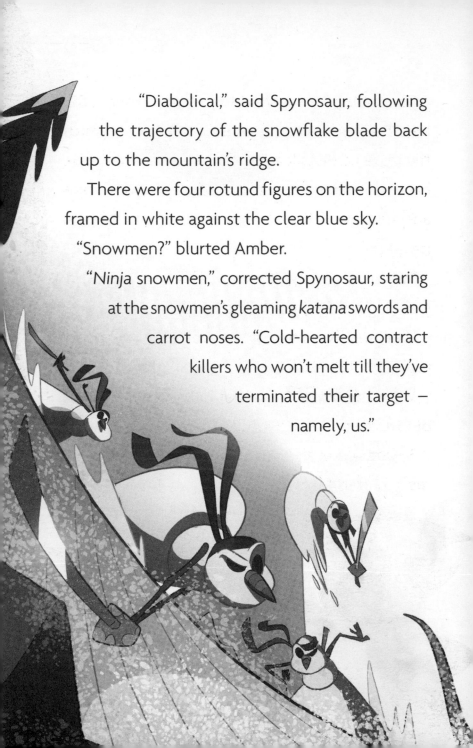

"Diabolical," said Spynosaur, following the trajectory of the snowflake blade back up to the mountain's ridge.

There were four rotund figures on the horizon, framed in white against the clear blue sky.

"Snowmen?" blurted Amber.

"*Ninja* snowmen," corrected Spynosaur, staring at the snowmen's gleaming *katana* swords and carrot noses. "Cold-hearted contract killers who won't melt till they've terminated their target — namely, us."

The snowmen began sliding towards them with breathtaking speed. Spynosaur glanced towards the maze of trees leading down the mountain. He handed Amber the attaché case. "He who spies and runs away, lives to spy another day. Get on my back!"

"What are you going to do?" Amber shrieked, grabbing hold of her dad's shoulders.

"I'm literally on top of the problem," Spynosaur replied. "Claw skis!"

With a **SHUFFF!** a pair of long, green skis shot out from beneath Spynosaur's feet.

"I want secret skis! How come I don't have secret skis?" huffed Amber.

"When you prove you can look after that new rabbit of yours, *then* you can have secret skis," replied her dad.

"I have proved it! Mr Fleming is— Yaah!" Amber shrieked as more deadly snowflakes whizzed past her head.

"Hang on – and don't let go of that case," said Spynosaur. He sped down the mountain, his skis carving through the snow as he aimed for the maze of trees.

Amber ducked as they raced under a low-hanging branch, with the ninja snowmen in hot pursuit. One of the snowmen bowed too late, and with a **FWUMP!** the branch knocked his head clean off. Spynosaur and Amber glanced back to see the snowman's body topple limply to the ground.

"If you can keep your head when all around you are losing theirs..." said Spynosaur with a smirk.

"One down, three to go!" cried Amber.

The remaining snowmen leaned backwards as they approached the branch, sliding under it in a stylish sub-zero limbo. Within moments they were gaining fast.

"They're still com— AAH!" screamed Amber as a snowflake blade skimmed past her head, slicing off a lock of hair.

"This calls for next-level impressiveness," noted Spynosaur. He turned his skis swiftly in the snow, spinning round to face the snowmen. As he sped backwards down the hill, narrowly avoiding tree after tree, Spynosaur drew his pistol.

"The heat ... is on," he said.

WHEN THE NINJA SNOWFLAKES FLY, THAT MIGHTY DINO'S GOING TO PROVE

THAT HE'S THE BACKWARDS-SKIING SUPER SPY WHO'S ALWAYS ON THE MOVE!

NOTHING'S GOING TO STOP HIM 'COS HE'S NEVER GOING TO STOP

BUT UNLESS HE TURNS ROUND QUICKLY, HE WON'T NOTICE THAT BIG DROP.

SPYNoSAUUUUUR!

"Well, the reception was a little *frosty* at first, but I think they *warmed* to me in the end," said Spynosaur, as the last of the ninja snowmen ground to a slushy halt.

"Da-ad," began Amber. "Would you please stop with the p— AAAH!"

The cliff edge came without warning. Spynosaur and Amber found themselves falling through the air. As they spun and spiralled, Amber saw the ground far below. Craggy rock jutted from beneath a covering of snow.

"We're going to **SPLAAAAAAT!**" she howled.

"Don't worry, I've got you – and dinosaurs always land on their feet!" said Spynosaur, his eyes flashing with a confident glint.

"That's *cats!*" shrieked Amber as the ground rushed towards them.

"Is it?" said Spynosaur. "Oh, dear."

5.
OH, DEER

"Owww," groaned Amber, dragging herself out of the snow. As she got to her feet, still clinging on to the attaché case, she was surprised to find herself in one piece. "Dad..."

"Don't panic – it takes more than a fall from a great height on to ragged rocks to stop your old dad."

Amber spun round to see Spynosaur leaning against a tree. She looked up to see the top of the cliff, obscured by cloud.

"We fell forever!" Amber cried. "How are we not completely dead?"

"It's really very simple," replied her dad. "As we plummeted to certain death, I— Oh, deer!"

"What is it?" asked Amber.

"No, not dear ... *deer*," replied Spynosaur.

In a clearing in the woods stood a red deer with great, branching antlers. Its ears pricked at the sound of the explosion, hot breath puffing out of its nose.

"HUNGRY..." snarled Spynosaur, his yellow eyes narrowing. **"RRRRRRR..."**

"Dad...?" said Amber, but it was too late. Her dad already had *that look* and Amber knew it well. His long, reptilian tongue licked around his mouth. He let out a low, ravenous rumble and gnashed his teeth.

"Oh, no," Amber sighed.

Don't give in to your dino-side!"

But Spynosaur wasn't listening. He hunched his back, ready to pounce.

"Dad!" Amber said again. "Please don't make me do it, please don't make me do it, please don't make me do it..."

roared Spynosaur, leaping into the air faster than a cobra. He raced towards the startled deer, which immediately broke into a panicked sprint. Spynosaur gnashed his jaws, gaining fast. Amber howled with frustration.

"Fine!" she cried. Then she took a deep breath ... and *sang*.

"I'm a little teapot, short and stout,
Here's my handle, here's my spout..."

Spynosaur's jaws suddenly snapped shut inches from the deer's neck. He skidded to a halt and turned to see a red-faced Amber, forming the shape of a teapot with her arms as she gently sang.

"When I get all steamed up, hear me shout,
Tip me up and pour me out!"

"RRRR...?" Spynosaur grunted, shaking his head.

"I'm a little teapot, short and stout,
Here's my handle, here's my spout,
When I get all steamed up, hear me—"

"RRraA—Amber! I ... I appear to be back," said Spynosaur, watching the panicked deer disappear into the trees. He ruffled his daughter's hair with a claw. "What would I do without my poppet? Only you seem to be able to purge me of my prehistoric rage..."

"Are you *sure* that stupid song is the only thing that works?" grumbled Amber, red-cheeked with humiliation.

"I'm afraid so," said Spynosaur. "It appears this new body is more than just a vessel for my astonishing brainwaves. I've ended up with what you so charmingly call my 'dino-side' ... the insatiable appetite of a hundred-million-year-old carnivore. For some reason, your timely tune is the only thing that brings me back to my senses."

"Well, don't let it happen again, 'cos I'm not *ever* doing that when there's other people around. It's the most embarrassing thing ever ... ever!" snarled Amber, still blushing. "I don't care if you eat all the fluffy animals in the world! I don't care if you eat the whole of Department 6 and Grandma on top! I don't care if you eat—"

"Hold that thought," said Spynosaur, checking his Super Secret Spy Watch™. "M11! Keeping busy?"

SPYNOSAUR! COME IN, SPYNOSAUR!

"Actually, I was taking bets with Newfangle about how much destruction you'd caused since this morning," M11 huffed.

"Things have rather gone off with a *bang*," Spynosaur confessed.

"Spynosaur, you maddening maverick!" tutted M11. "Must chaos and destruction follow you on every mission?"

"Not *every* mission..." said Spynosaur, sheepishly kicking the snow with a clawed foot.

"Oh really?" snapped M11. "What about:

MISSION #5 // YOU ONLY EXPLODE TWICE

DEPARTMENT **6**

MISSION #21 // DIAL 'D' FOR DEVASTATION

DEPARTMENT **6**

MISSION #41 // THE SPY WHO WENT BOOM

DEPARTMENT **6**

"They were one-offs … all three of them," Spynosaur noted, giving Amber a wink.

"But we found the McGuffin!" cried Amber, waving the case.

"Actually," began Spynosaur. "I said it *might* be the—"

"You have the McGuffin? Well, that changes everything! Excellent work, agents – return to headquarters immediately," said M11.

"Keep your moustache on, M11," said Spynosaur. "Danger Monkey is still missing and I'm not about to leave an agent out in the *cold*..."

"Blast it to smithereens, this is not open for debate – our priority is keeping the McGuffin out of the hands of P.O.I.S.O.N.," M11 snapped. "You may have no respect for rules, Spynosaur, but I wrote the book on them … or at least I edited the most recent edition. Now get your tail back to headquarters – that's an order!"

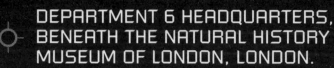

6.
ON THE CASE

**DEPARTMENT 6 HEADQUARTERS,
BENEATH THE NATURAL HISTORY
MUSEUM OF LONDON, LONDON.**

The Dino-soarer docked silently on the roof of London's Natural History Museum and dropped the scaly super-spy and his sidekick down the museum's chimney. With a **FWOOOOMP** they were swallowed into metallic tubes, which transported the pair at dizzying speed to the Department's underground headquarters.

"Spynosaur!" squealed a voice as the tubes deposited Spynosaur and Amber (still clutching the attaché case) in a wide, starkly lit room filled with banks of computers, doodads, thingamabobs and whatchamacallits. A distractingly tall man in a long white coat made a beeline for Spynosaur. He had wild hair that seemed to be trying to escape from his head, and glasses so thick that his eyes looked ready to explode.

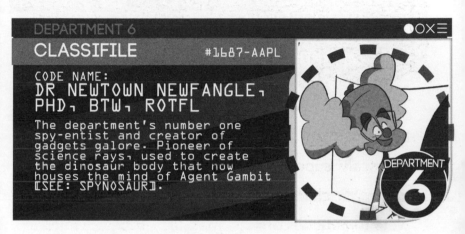

"And how is my greatest spy-entific triumph doing today?" continued Dr Newfangle, shining a torch into Spynosaur's large, lizard eyes. "Still functioning at maximum capacity?"

"I'm fine, Doctor ... if that's what you're asking," replied Spynosaur, as Newfangle began measuring his tail.

"And how are your motor functions? Balance? Claw-eye coordination?" Newfangle continued, poking and prodding Spynosaur with various spy-entific implements. "Any odd sensations? Any peculiar appetites?"

Spynosaur shot Amber a look.

"Do put him down, Newfangle," huffed M11 as she strode into the room, her moustache twitching. She pointed to the case held in Amber's hand. "The only important thing is to get *that* under lock and key ... and ensure that no one ever gets their hands on it."

"Out of the question," said Spynosaur. "We need to crack open the case and find out what's inside."

"*Open* it? Are you mad?" howled M11. "The McGuffin is a super-secret weapon! It could blow us to smithereens!"

"Or shrink us to the size of insects!" added Newfangle.

"Or release a fog that brain-melts us into blank-eyed, slobbbery, face-chewing zombies!" cried Amber.

"No more late night TV for you, poppet," said her dad. "Look, Ego *wanted* us to find the McGuffin. He's playing a game with us ... and I don't like games. Except KerPlunk."

"Uh, Dad? Something's ... happening," said Amber.

Everyone turned to see the case rattle and shake in her hands.

"It's going to blow!" shrieked M11. "Smithereens for everyone!"

"I don't think so..." said Spynosaur, taking the rattling case from his daughter.

"Spynosaur!" yelled M11. "What are you going to—? Don't you dare!"

"'Dare' is my middle name ... I changed it from 'Simon'," said Spynosaur – and sank his teeth into the lock with a **KRUNCH!**

7.
DANGER MONKEY

"WAAA–O–O–AAH!"

A moment after Spynosaur tore the lock off the attaché case with his teeth, the case sprang open – and out leaped a screaming monkey dressed in a black spy-suit.

"*Danger Monkey?*" blurted Spynosaur as the monkey latched on to Spynosaur's face and began pummelling it with tiny fists.

PAP-AP-AP-AP!

"Lock me up, willya?" screamed the monkey madly. "I'll knock yer teeth into next-door's garden! I'll slap yer socks inside out! I'll judo-toss yer legs over yer neck!"

With a shake of his great head, Spynosaur flung Danger Monkey across the room. The monkey bounced along the ground before leaping to his feet again.

"I'll play xylophone on yer funny bone! I'll chew on yer fatty bits! I'll stub yer toe!" Danger Monkey howled. Then he reached his hand behind his back. "I'll— I'll— **WAOOAH!**"

"Umm," began Amber. "Is he about to do what I think he's about to—"

"He's got a whole handful!" shrieked Newfangle. "And he's not afraid to use it!"

"Duck and cover!" M11 barked.

"Danger Monkey, stop!" Spynosaur cried. "You may have had your brainwaves transferred into the body of a spider monkey following an unfortunate incident with a punctured parachute and a pool of piranhas, but that doesn't mean you should give in to animal instincts!"

Amber was panicking that her dad would ask her to sing *that* song to calm the monkey down, when:

"S-Spyno? Spyno, me ol' china!" Danger Monkey suddenly cried, pausing mid-toss. "Sorry 'bout losin' me cool back there – I thought you was Ergo Ego. That pain in the tail locked me up in there..."

"Why would Ego lock you in a case?" asked Amber.

The monkey squared up to her. "You callin' me a liar? Tryin' to make a monkey outta me?" he growled, brandishing his handful of excrement. "I'll dip me tail in chilli sauce and stick it in yer ear!"

"Enough! Report, Danger Monkey!" barked M11. "What happened to you?"

"Ego rumbled me, Boss ... he caught me mid-spy," explained Danger Monkey, clearly irked.

"He tempted me inside that case with a nice, juicy banana. Stinkin' fruit must've been drugged, 'cos next thing I know, I'm waking up in the dark. Curse me uncontrollable cravin' for bananas!" He glared at Newfangle. "I s'pose that's what comes with 'avin' yer brainwaves put into a *monkey* instead of a *dinosaur*..."

"For the last time, Danger Monkey, I had no choice!" insisted Newfangle. "It's not easy growing a dinosaur, even with the almost limitless power of the Science Ray ... not to mention trying to *retro-engineer* Ergo Ego's brain-box technology. But rest assured, just because you are not a dinosaur does not make you any less extraordinary. Allow me to explain, in the best way I know..."

"Not this again, Newfangle!" growled M11. "We don't have time for your—"

Newfangle pressed a button on the wall and it slid aside to reveal a brightly lit stage, complete with a microphone stand and backing dancers in white coats. Newfangle hopped on to the stage, and so began:

DR NEWFANGLE'S SUPER SPY-ENCE RAP

Science? **Science?** Make way for **spy-ence!**
Here comes the news to throw the
doubters into silence!
Made a **dinosaur** with my super-science rays
Add a slice of spy with the help of brainy-waves
Zap! Zap! I just made your day!

Blazin' a new trail
with a trace of DNA

I'm Evolutin' man – got a
super-spy-ence plan

Made a dinosaur a spy!

He's so fly!

Check it, Spynosaur's
the MAN!

"Blast it to smithereens! Have you quite finished, Doctor?" snapped M11.

"So you see, Danger Monkey? Spy-ence made you super-special!" added Newfangle, dropping the mic and hopping down from the stage.

"Special? What are you talkin' about? That was just about how awesome dinosaurs are! Monkeys don't even get a mention!" screeched Danger Monkey, holding his fistful of foulness aloft. "I've got a good mind to fling this right in your—"

"Um, I don't mean to interrupt," Amber interrupted. "But is your poo ... flashing?"

Everyone's eyes darted to Danger Monkey's hand. Sure enough, the handful of excrement was blinking with a faint red light.

"Well spotted, poppet," said Spynosaur. He cautiously reached a claw into the poo and pulled out a small piece of plastic, illuminated at one end by a flashing light.

"Who put that in there?" growled Danger Monkey. "Nobody messes with my mess!"

"It's a data drive ... hidden inside that drugged banana you ate, no doubt," said Spynosaur, carrying it at arm's length over to a bank of computers. He plugged it in. An image appeared simultaneously on every screen in the room.

"Ergo Ego!" cried Amber. The egg-shaped head of their arch-enemy loomed large on the screens.

"Is this recording?" Ego began. "I can never work these things... Do I have to press something? You would think an evil genius could fathom how to— Wait, wait, I've got it. OK..." Ergo Ego sat back in his chair and cleared his throat. "Greetings, dummies of Department 6! So, I bet you totally thought the McGuffin was in that attaché case, didn't you?

HDMI 2 EEGO 2GB

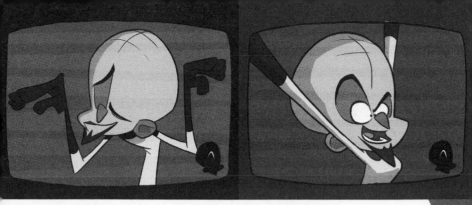

I bet you were all, 'Hey, we totally found the super-secret weapon! I can't believe Ego just left it here – what a stupid head!' But no! It is your heads that are stupid!"

"What you sayin' about my 'ead?" growled Danger Monkey. "I'll boil-wash your underpants and give you a wedgie! I'll break out me watercolours an' paint an unflatterin' portrait of ya!"

"Quiet!" insisted M11. "Ego may be about to needlessly explain his next move!"

"But ... since you are so keen to find the real super-secret weapon, I have arranged a demonstration of its power," Ego continued. "Tonight the world will witness my McGuffin in all its glory! And you won't even know until it's too late, you stupid heads!"

The screen went black.

"What are we going to do?" said Amber. "He could be anywhere in the world! How do we know where he's going to—"

"Venice, Italy," said Spynosaur. "*That's* where Ego plans to unleash his weapon."

"How'd you work that out?" said Danger Monkey, scratching his head, among other things.

"It's very simple ... from the tone of his voice, Ego's mouth was numb from cold – a clear sign that he's been eating ice cream," explained Spynosaur. "Ice cream goes well with cheesecake. Cheesecake contains no cheese. 'No cheese' sounds like 'Noches', which is 'night' in Spanish. In Spain, the rain falls mainly on the plain. 'Plain' crisps are merely salted. Salt is accompanied by its less popular counterpart, pepper. 'Pepper' makes you sneeze. The longest sneezing spree lasted nine hundred and seventy-eight days. And nine hundred

and seventy-
eight is the favourite
number of the King of Italy ... who
is hosting a masquerade ball
at his grand palace tonight.
A perfectly public place for
Ego to unleash his McGuffin."

"Wait... What?" said Amber.

"You're right, poppet, it's almost too
obvious – I barely had to use my spy skills at
all," added Spynosaur. "It's as if Ego wanted us to
know his plans ... but why?"

"There's no time to question the whys and
wherefores," interrupted M11. "Ergo Ego's going to
unleash his McGuffin, Spynosaur. What are you
going to do about it?"

Spynosaur raised a scaly eyebrow. "Save the
day, of course," he said. "Now somebody get me a
cocktail dress..."

8.
DINOSAUR IN DISGUISE

 THE GRAND PALACE OF VENICE, VENICE, ITALY.

The grand palace's ballroom was vast, with marble floors and chandelier-covered ceilings as far as the eye could see. It teemed with guests dressed in finery and ornate masks, all boasting about how rich and shiny-haired they were. At the far end of the ballroom stood the King of Italy, dressed in a gold tuxedo and an elaborate crown, which doubled his height. The king regaled his guests with tales of his eminence and sipped pink champagne through a solid gold straw. Standing in the doorway at the other end of the ballroom, Amber adjusted the black mask that covered her eyes.

"So, what's the plan?" she whispered.

"The plan is to stick to the plan," said M11's voice in Amber's earpiece. "Danger Monkey is covering the building from the outside. You two split up and look for the McGuffin. And for goodness' sake, remember you're spies – you don't have to blow everything up. Try to keep a low profile."

Amber looked up at her dad. He was wearing a long black dress squeezed over his huge, scaly frame, a blonde wig on his head, long white gloves and high-heeled shoes over his great clawed feet. He took a glossy red lipstick out of his handbag and painted it round his mouth.

"Low profile," repeated Amber. "Right."

"Let's save the day, shall we?" said Spynosaur, raising a feathered mask to his face.

"Bet I can find the McGuffin before you!" declared Amber. She hurried inside and up a grand sweeping stairwell, keen to get a bird's-eye view of the ballroom.

"That's my girl," said Spynosaur proudly. Then he straightened his wig and slipped into the crowd of masked revellers, his long dress and even longer tail swishing behind him.

"I spy with my little eye..." he said. "Something beginning with—"

"You!"

"No, not U..." muttered Spynosaur, spinning round.

The crowds duly parted as the portly shape of the King of Italy waddled towards him. He halted in Spynosaur's shadow and peered up at him, his eyes wide.

"It cannot be... You're ... you're..." he uttered. "You're the most enchanting creature I have ever seen, Madame!"

"I am?" Spynosaur replied, pressing the mask to his face. In a high-pitched voice he replied, "Uh, I mean, most kind, Your Majesty."

"I don't believe we have been introduced," the king continued, holding out his hand. "I am the King of Italy. And you are...?"

"Yes, I am," Spynosaur replied coyly, holding out a huge gloved hand.

The king kissed it excitedly. "Such a beguiling enchantress!" he said. Then he grabbed a glass of champagne from a passing waiter and drank it in one gulp. "May I have this dance?" he asked.

"Dance?" Spynosaur replied, fanning himself with his mask. "Oh, I'm afraid I don't—"

"Then I shall teach you, Madame!" interrupted the king. "I shall teach you!"

Amber had barely reached the top of the stairs before she glanced down and saw her father being spun around the dance floor by an old man with a golden crown.

"Oh, *no*. Da-ad...!" she groaned.

"What he's done this time?" said M11 through the earpiece. "Blast it all to smithereens, he can't have blown up the palace already..."

"Worse – he's *dancing*," Amber sighed. "Dads

should never, *ever*— Huh?"

Amber glanced up to the top of the stairs. A tall, slender woman in a black robe and pointy hat swept across her path and down the corridor.

"I spy with my little eye..." she said suspiciously. She looked back to see her dad busily doing pirouettes with the King of Italy. Then she took a deep breath and raced after the woman.

9.
KILLS WITCH

Amber pursued the woman in the black robe to the end of the corridor. The woman moved like a shadow, sweeping inside a room on the first floor directly above the ballroom. Amber followed as spy-lently as she could. The room was filled with crates, boxes, and piles of trinkets.

Amber hid behind a crate as she watched the woman draw a silver attaché case from her robes. It was identical to the one they had recovered from Ego's hideout – the McGuffin had to be inside. The woman opened the case, carefully removed a metallic black sphere and twisted it in both hands until it clicked. Amber heard an ominous **TICK–**

TOCK-ing and saw a countdown light up on the face of the sphere.

00:00:59

"The McGuffin!" gasped Amber in a whisper.

The robed woman spun round. Amber slapped her hands over her mouth. After a moment, the woman returned to the task in hand.

00:00:55

The woman placed the sphere on one of the crates. She tilted her head slowly to one side, her eyes flashing red. It was only then that Amber caught sight of her metallic, skull-like face. She recognized it immediately.

DEPARTMENT 6

CLASSIFILE   #1984-DZ-M11

CODE NAME: KILLS WITCH

>> Ruthless robot-for-hire /
automated assassin, constantly
looking to upgrade her hardware.
Armed to her metallic teeth with
state-of-the-art weaponry.

"Oi!" Amber cried, leaping out and striking a battle-ready pose. "Step away from that super-secret weapon, Kills Witch!"

Kills Witch spun round, flinging her robe disguise to the floor to reveal a slender metallic body, with a laser cannon in place of her left arm.

"Uh-oh," muttered Amber as Kills Witch fired.

A bolt of blue energy blasted from the barrel, and the floor beneath Amber's feet disintegrated. She fell, plunging to the ballroom below.

"AAH!" she screamed. Then, "Huh?"

Amber had stopped falling. She'd landed on a huge chandelier, suspended high above the ballroom. Far below her was her dad, still dancing with the King of Italy.

"Dad!" Amber cried. Spynosaur looked up, mid-pirouette.

"Amber?" he said. "Hang on!"

"Dad, Kills Witch is here!" Amber yelled, clinging on to the chandelier as it swung. "And she's set the McGuffin to go off in hardly any seconds!"

00:00:31

"What's the meaning of this?" the king asked.

"Forgive me, Your Majesty, I'm going to have to sit out the next dance," said Spynosaur, nodding to the King of Italy. With that, he spun the king so fast that he was sent careering into a sculpture of himself made from gold jelly.

00:00:20

"Dad! It's giving way!" Amber cried as the ceiling buckled under the chandelier's added weight.

Spynosaur tore off his dress to reveal his sleek spy suit. From his holster he drew a large pistol with a silver grappling hook attached to the barrel.

"Spynosaur! Report!" M11 bellowed in his earpiece. "Danger Monkey said he heard gunfire! What's happening in there?"

"Just *grappling* with a few issues, M11," said Spynosaur.

With a **SHOOOF** the grappling hook shot upwards as the chandelier — and Amber — fell. The hook whizzed past Amber's head, embedding itself with a **THUNK** in the ceiling. Spynosaur hung on as he retracted the grapple, pulling himself up into the air. He flew past the chandelier at speed, grabbing Amber in his spare hand and swinging her effortlessly on to his back.

00:00:15

Seconds later the chandelier smashed against the marble floor, sending the revellers running for cover as a thousand sparkling shards flew across the room.

00:00:13

And seconds after *that*, Spynosaur smashed through the hole in the ceiling, emerging in the store room above and landing in a suitably dramatic pose.

00:00:10

"You must be saving for another upgrade, Kills Witch ... and I'll bet Ergo Ego was the highest bidder for your cybernetic services," said Spynosaur, flashing his sharp teeth. "May I have this dance?"

10.
NINE SECONDS

"It's been ages since I destroyed you last, Kills Witch," Spynosaur said, as Amber climbed down from his back. "I see you've built another body. You know, you could just stop being evil and I'd leave you alone."

00 : 00 : 08

"Don't---*klik*---blame---me---blame---my---*klik*---programming," the robot said as sarcastically as a robot might.

"Spynosaur, report!" barked M11 into his earpiece. "I'm getting word that the King of Italy has been thrown into a jelly sculpture of himself! What's going on? Have you found the McGuffin?"

00:00:07

"We have to turn it off!" Amber cried. "There's only seconds left before the McGuffin does whatever it's going to do!"

00:00:06

"You---*klik*---want---it? Come---and---*klik*---get---it," said the robot, raising her formidable arm cannon.

Spynosaur fired his grapple gun, clamping on to Kills Witch's metallic chest plate. He yanked the grapple as she fired, throwing off her aim. The blast seared past them. Amber felt the heat of the laser as it disintegrated the wall behind them.

"Things are *hotting* up a little here, M11," confessed Spynosaur. "But it's nothing we can't handle!"

Spynosaur wrenched the grapple gun again, pulling Kills Witch into the air towards him – and swung his mighty tail. It smashed into her with the force of at least three normal dinosaur tails, sending her crashing into a pile of spare royal crowns.

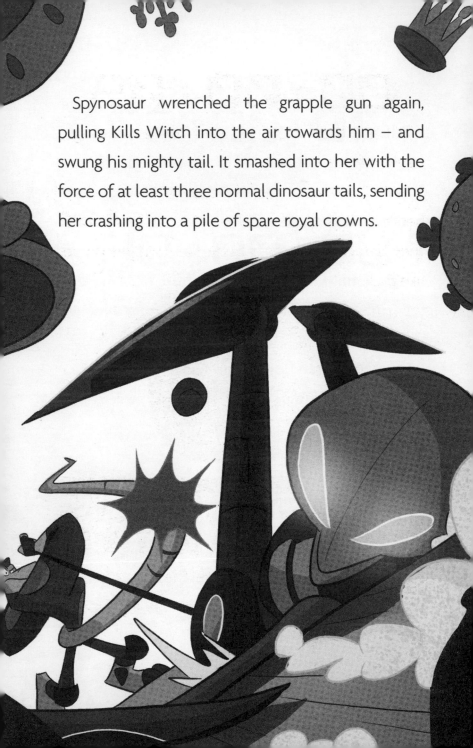

00:00:05

"I'll get the McGuffin!" said Amber, making a beeline for the sphere.

"Wait!" Spynosaur yelled. He saw Kills Witch point her long legs at his sidekick. With a **FWOOSH!** they detached from her body, launching at Amber like rockets.

"Amber!" cried Spynosaur. **"UNPREDICTABLE GUSTY GIBBON HANDS OF STUBBORN IRONING BOARD DEFENCE!"**

"Huh?" Amber turned to see the jet-propelled legs blasting towards her and her training flashed before her eyes...

ONE YEAR AGO

ERGO EGO'S SECRET ISLAND LAIR, THE BERMUDA TRIANGLE.

That was ... wow. WOW, Dad! You beat the baddies with your bare hands!

I was fairly exceptional, wasn't I? Did you notice when I got that big one in a headlock and— Wait, that's not the point!

You shouldn't even be here, poppet! What on earth were you thinking, stowing away in my luggage before I set off on my secret mission to Ergo Ego's secret island lair?

I was trying to prove what I'd already worked out, Dad! You're a *spy* ... and I want to be a spy, too! Spying's the best thing *ever*. Better than chips or cake or dinosaurs!

Being a spy isn't just incredibly awesome ... it's dangerous. You can't just become one overnight. There's *training* and all sorts.

I can do training! I have ninja skills!

AND BACK IN THE PRESENT...

"UNPREDICTABLE GUSTY GIBBON HANDS OF STUBBORN IRONING BOARD DEFENCE!" cried Amber,

echoing her dad's command.

CHONG!
CHANG!

With breathtaking speed and skill, Amber deflected the jet-propelled rocket legs, sending them crashing to the ground in a flurry of lightning-fast movement.

"Didn't I tell you? It happens more often than you might think," said Spynosaur.

00 : 00 : 03

"Dad, the McGuffin!" Amber shouted. "Time's almost up!"

"Don't worry, poppet ... as any secret agent worth his or her salt will tell you, the key to this sort of thing, without a doubt, is timing," said Spynosaur. "I can honestly say, claw on heart, that I've never met a super-secret weapon I couldn't disarm at the last second, no matter how long—"

"Dad!" screamed Amber.

"Oh yes, quite right," noted Spynosaur. He picked up the sphere in his claws and turned it. It made a loud *BEEEEEP* and a click ... freezing the timer at

"See?" Spynosaur added.

"Is it me, or did that nine seconds last a *really* long time?" Amber said, blowing on her sore hands. "How did we not get blown to bits?"

"It's really very simple—" Spynosaur began.

"Dad!" Amber interrupted.

Spynosaur turned to see the legless remains of Kills Witch spring on to her arms and propel herself through a window, plunging with a **POSSSSSH** into the canal below.

Spynosaur and Amber raced over to the smashed window and looked down to see Kills Witch emerge from the water, her torso now plugged into what looked like a huge metallic fish.

"*Getaway shark*," snarled Spynosaur. "Diabolical."

"She's getting away! We've got to stop her!" declared Amber, but within seconds Kills Witch was halfway down the canal, the robotic shark's motors slicing through the water at high speed.

"Let her go, agents," M11 ordered through

their earpieces. "Our main priority is getting the McGuffin back to headquarters so we can lock it away forever."

"Not this time," growled Spynosaur, tucking the McGuffin into his spy suit. "Ego's still out there, and I'll bet real money Kills Witch knows where..."

Spynosaur put two clawed fingers into his mouth and let out a whistle so shrill it shattered the palace's windows.

"Somebody call for a taxi?" said a voice.

Amber looked left and saw a sleek, night-black speedboat draw up underneath them, with Danger Monkey at the controls. He revved the engines. "Who fancies a spot of high-speed pursuit?"

11.
JUMPING
THE
SHARK

RUN ALL YOU LIKE
BUT THERE'S A DINO ON YOUR TAIL

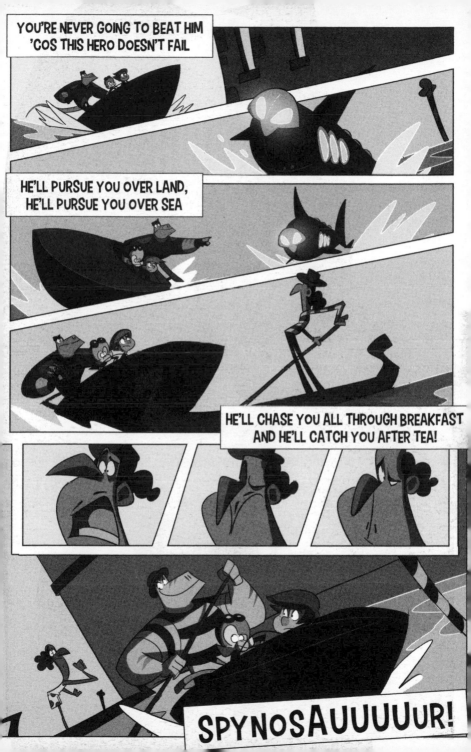

"Come back 'ere, y'rotten robot! I'm gonna twist yer earlobes!" cried Danger Monkey.

"Move over, Danger Monkey, I'll *steer* us in the right direction," said Spynosaur, pushing Danger Monkey aside and grabbing the controls.

"Oi! Just 'cos I'm three feet tall and exist primarily on a diet of fruit and small insects, don't mean I'm useless!" he complained.

Spynosaur ignored him, piloting the jet-powered speedboat across the usually calm water of the Venice canals.

"That way! Turn!" cried Amber, following the wake of Kills Witch's robotic getaway shark.

Spynosaur heaved the controls and the speedboat banked right, pursuing the shark under a bridge – and straight towards a brick wall. It was a dead end.

"There's nowhere to run, Kills Witch!" Spynosaur smirked.

Kills Witch spun her getaway shark round to face them. The cybernetic sorceress's eyes glowed red and the engines of the getaway shark roared ... then she headed straight towards them.

"She's playin' chicken!" cried Danger Monkey as she zoomed ever closer. "Back up, Spyno!"

"No, I don't think so," said Spynosaur. Then he released the controls, and folded his arms.

The speedboat slowed to a stop.

"Um, Dad?" said Amber as the getaway shark sped at them on a collision course. "What are you doing?"

"You know, when Dr Newfangle was building this speedboat, I remember saying there was one trick we couldn't live without," replied Spynosaur.

"What – what trick?" asked Amber.

Kills Witch was only a moment from collision.

"Vertical take-off," replied Spynosaur. He hit a button on the control panel and the speedboat launched straight up into the air, blasted skywards with boat-bottom rockets. As the getaway shark roared underneath, Spynosaur reached a great claw over the side of the airborne speedboat. He wrapped it round Kills Witch's head and tore it from her shoulders.

"It's so easy to *lose your head* in these situations," said Spynosaur, as the speedboat slammed back on to the surface of the water. Amber turned to see the getaway shark swim helplessly into a wall, exploding into a thousand robotic pieces.

"Terrible pun aside, that was awesome," she said.

"This---isn't---over," said Kills Witch's head. "The---real---McGuffin---is---still---*klik*---out---there."

"Where? Where is it? Tell me! Where is the real—" growled Spynosaur, just as the robot's head opened with a whirr.

"Brain bomb!" growled Spynosaur. Less than a second later, Kills Witch's rigged-to-explode cranium went...

BOOM!

12.
A BUMP ON THE HEAD

◎ **No.13 DIGGLE DRIVE, THE VILLAGE OF LITTLE WALLOP**

"Dad!" Amber cried out, sitting upright. She came face to face with her mum, looking back at her with concern.

"How are you feeling?" said Amber's mum. Amber glanced around. She was lying on her bed. Back in her room. Back at home.

"Mum? Wait, what?" she muttered. She rubbed her head. Her room was just as she'd left it. On her bedside table was her toy shop-bought spy diary and spy pen. On her shelf were all her favourite books – *How to Spot a Secret Agent, A Spy's Guide to Keeping Secrets, I, Spy/You Spy* ... and in the corner of her room her pet rabbit, Mr Fleming, shuffled around his hutch.

"How did I get here?" Amber asked.

"Apparently you took a tumble in the playground," said her mum. "Do you remember? You've got a nasty bump on the head. The school thought it was best if you came home."

"They did...?" Amber muttered. She checked her head and, sure enough, found a lump on it the size of a ping-pong ball. Then she saw a long, scaly tail poking out from inside her wardrobe. "Oh," she added. "*Right.*"

"You get yourself comfy – I'll make you a sandwich," said Amber's mum. "Then I think you should get some sleep."

With that, Amber's mum trotted out of the bedroom and downstairs.

"You can come out, she's gone," Amber said.

At the far end of her room, Amber's wardrobe

door creaked open and Spynosaur all but fell out.

"You should really tidy up in there, it looks like something exploded," he said, plucking a sock from the ridge of his nose.

"Never mind that – what happened?" Amber asked.

"Ah, yes. When Kills Witch's head blew up you were blown backwards... Knocked yourself out on the boat," Spynosaur explained. "I thought it was better to get you home and let you sleep it off."

"It is good you are not dead. Today I was back of cow in school play," said Sergei, suddenly appearing from behind Amber's curtain. He took off his wig with a sigh. "You will be at school tomorrow, yes? You have maths test."

"Uh, sorry, Sergei," said Amber with a shrug. "I'm pretty sure I'm saving the world tomorrow."

"Suit yourself," Sergei huffed. Then he leaped out of Amber's window and disappeared into the night.

Amber rubbed her head.

"I'm sorry, poppet, I should have seen Kills Witch's exploding-head trick coming," said Spynosaur. "Although it could have been worse – poor Danger Monkey's going to have his tail in plaster for a month."

"But we saved the day, though, right?" said Amber.

Spynosaur let out a frustrated growl. Then he opened his claw to reveal a familiar black sphere.

"The McGuffin...?" Amber said.

"...Is nothing more than a fancy egg-timer – look," Spynosaur said. He gripped the sphere in both claws and turned it. It split in two with a **POP!**

Both halves were empty.

"I don't get it – if it's not a super-secret weapon, why would Ego go to all that trouble and hire a killer robot and stuff?" asked Amber, her mind racing. "Why the tick-tock and the countdown if nothing was going to happen? What's the point?"

"I ... don't know," replied Spynosaur.

Amber could tell it was a hard thing for her dad to admit — he always knew everything. She watched him pace around the room, his great tail swishing from side to side. "All I do know is that Ergo Ego's been playing us from the start," he continued. "But there's something to this McGuffin business I'm not seeing ... something diabolical. And not knowing is making me ... *hungry*."

"I know what you mean; it doesn't— Wait, 'hungry'?" said Amber. She saw her dad looming over her rabbit with *that* look in his eyes.

HUNGRY..." Spynsoaur snarled.

"Dad, no! Not Mr Fleming! You got me that bunny!" said Amber ... but it was too late. Spynosaur was licking his lips and grinding his razor-sharp teeth ... lost to his dino-side.

"Great ... just great," Amber grumbled, clambering out of bed. "But if Mum hears me singing, we're all in trouble..."

Two verses of
"I'm a Little Teapot"
later...

"I appear to be back," said Spynosaur as Amber cradled her terrified rabbit in her arms, red-faced at having to sing *that* song, even in front of her pet. "What would I do without my poppet?"

"For the last time, stop calling me that!" Amber huffed. "And what about poor Mr Fleming? You scared him half to death..."

"My sincerest apologies, Mr Fleming," Spynosaur added meekly. Then he headed for the window and began climbing out.

"Dad?" said Amber. "Ego's super-secret weapon ... it's still out there, isn't it?"

Spynosaur took a deep breath. "Yes, I believe it is," he said. "So get some rest. We've got a big day tomorrow. We're saving the world."

Spynosaur disappeared through her window. Amber put Mr Fleming back in his cage and climbed into bed. She lay her head on the pillow and closed her eyes.

"Saving the world," she whispered. Then she thought spy thoughts until she fell asleep.

13.
McGUFFINS GALORE

WEDNESDAY 09:19

 ## THE PYRAMIDS, CAIRO, EGYPT

"Is *this* what you meant by 'we've got a big day tomorrow'?" asked Amber. She and her dad were clinging on to the landing skids of a helicopter as it soared over the deserts of Egypt.

"Admit it, it's not every morning you see a helicopter take off through the top of a pyramid!" roared Spynosaur over the whirling din of the 'copter's rotor blades. "Good job we were able to leap on to it at the last minute..."

Good morning, stupid heads of Department 6! This is an anonamoss ... aminomiss— aninnanoss ... secret tip-off. Ergo Ego, the incredibly awesome international criminal, who is also ever so charming and funny and actually taller than he looks, is planning to transport his super-secret weapon from his hideout-stroke-holiday-home in Egypt. If you want to stop him, follow these coordinates ... and perhaps you will finally solve the riddle of the McGuffin. You stupid heads!

"Couldn't we just have followed it in the Dino-soarer?" howled Amber, clinging on for dear life.

"A secret agent should start every day with an act of reckless daring. And perhaps a spot of yoga," replied Spynosaur. "Now hang on!"

Spynosaur climbed up the landing skids and dug his clawed hand into the cabin door, before wrenching it open with an almighty heave. The pilot turned to see the huge dinosaur peering back at him, teeth bared.

"Get," growled Spynosaur, "OUT."

"AAAAAAH!"

screamed the pilot, diving out of the other side of the 'copter. Spynosaur climbed inside and grabbed the controls.

"How's the cargo?" asked Amber, clambering up the skids and joining her dad inside the 'copter. She saw a large crate in the centre of the cargo bay. It was filled to the brim with a hundred identical black metal spheres.

"McGuffins! McGuffins galore!" Amber gasped, her eyes wide. "But which one is the super-secret weapon?"

"First the 'anonymous' tip-off and now this! It's more of Ergo Ego's gameplay," snarled a frustrated Spynosaur. "But why would he—? Wait."

Spynosaur squinted. Taped to the dashboard of the helicopter was a sealed letter, with "Spynosaur" written neatly upon the envelope.

"I know that handwriting..." he growled.

"What is it?" asked Amber.

Spynosaur tore open the letter and unfolded it.

Dear Spynosaur,

Hi again! Long time no correspond. You know, people don't write enough letters ... it's a dying art.

Oh, and speaking of **dying**, you have about thirty seconds to live.

The antidote is hidden inside one of these many fake McGuffins. If you survive, which you will not, I will show you how to find my **real** super-secret weapon.

Good luck!
You *stupid* head.

Yours sincerely,
ergo eyo

"What's he on about? What antidote?" said Amber.

Spynosaur's lizard eyes narrowed. He held up the letter and sniffed it.

"It's a *poisoned-pen letter!*" Spynosaur growled.

He scrunched the letter in his claw and looked at his ink-stained fingers. "The ink is a deadly neuro-toxin, absorbed through the skin. Ego ... tricked us ... again. *Dia ... bol ... ical...*"

"You all right, Dad? You look even greener than usual," asked Amber.

Spynosaur shook his head as if trying to stay awake, beads of sweat appearing on his scaly brow.

"Antidote ... inside ... one of ... McGuffins..." he gasped, tapping his Super Secret Spy Watch™ with a clawed finger. "Thirty ... seconds ... to live..."

"*Thirty seconds?*" Amber howled. Her father was already swaying woozily from side to side.

Amber raced over to the crate and grabbed one of the spheres. She gripped it in both hands and turned it. It opened with a **POP!** ... but there was nothing inside.

"How do I know which one to choose?" yelled Amber, popping open sphere after sphere – but finding nothing inside. "Dad! How do I know?"

"S'all right..." slurred Spynosaur. "I have ... a plan..."

"What plan?" screamed Amber. She turned to see her dad slump forward against the release lever for the cargo door.

VRRRR!

Amber let out a squeak as the helicopter's cargo door swung open.

A second later she, Spynosaur and the crate of McGuffin spheres were sucked out into the air.

14.
FALLING, LANDING AND EVERYTHING IN BETWEEN

Amber found herself plummeting towards the desert alongside Spynosaur and a hundred black spheres, as the now pilot-less helicopter spiralled out of control above them.

"This is not 'a plan'! This is just falling!" she screamed. She remembered her dad once telling her that the best thing to do when you only have seconds to live is to find a way not to die. That, or hug a loved one. With the ground rushing up to meet them, she decided to do both. She tucked in her arms and dived like an arrow towards the limp, spiralling body of her father. She darted past sphere after sphere, edging steadily closer

until she was near enough to touch him.
Then, in the split-second between being
smacked by a flailing tail or a
claw, she managed to grab her
dad's back and cling on for
dear life.

"Dad!" Amber howled.
"Find a way not to die!"

"Wuurrhh?" grunted
Spynosaur, his eyes
opening a crack and
looking around.
Then, with the
last of his strength,
Spynosaur pointed
a claw towards
one of the black
spheres. "I ... spy ...
that one..."

"That one? Why that one?" cried Amber as her dad passed out. Amber grunted in frustration. She gripped his shoulders and aimed them towards the sphere. By now the pyramids loomed large beneath them – the ground was fast approaching. Amber held her breath, guiding them expertly through the air. She stretched out a hand and grabbed the sphere. "Got it! Hang on, Dad!"

Amber twisted the sphere, which opened with a **POP!** Nestled inside was a small syringe of red liquid. Without thinking, she pulled it out and jabbed it hard into her dad's scaly neck.

"Dad, I did it!" she said. "What now?"

Amber glanced over his shoulder. All she could see was the ground – they were moments from impact.

"Huh," she muttered. "I guess we don't get to save the world, after all."

Amber hugged her dad close. Then she closed her eyes and waited for the end.

Then she waited a bit longer.

And a bit longer.

Then she opened her eyes.

"Whuh?" she exclaimed. She and her father were hovering, suspended, a few inches from the ground. Amber turned, looked up and saw the familiar shimmer of the almost-invisible Dino-soarer. It had them firmly caught in its gravity beam.

She turned and saw her dad pointing weakly at his Super Secret Spy Watch™.

"Told you ... I had ... a plan," he muttered.

As the gravity beam deposited them gently on to the Egyptian sand, Spynosaur yawned as if waking up from a restorative nap.

"That antidote's working a treat — nicely done, poppet," he said, stretching out his arms and tail. "Between your quick-thinking and my activating the Dino-soarer's autopilot with my Super Secret Spy Watch™, thus saving us from certain splat, I'd say we're back on track."

"What just happened?" said a flabbergasted Amber, looking around at the dozens of black spheres which were strewn across the desert. "There were a hundred fake McGuffins falling through the air — how could you have known which one contained the antidote?"

"It's really very simple," Spynosaur began. "You see, I— *Wait.*"

Something had caught Spynosaur's eye. Amber followed her father's gaze across the desert. Towering over the landscape lay the Great Sphinx, a statue of a vast stone lion with a woman's head. It was bigger than any house Amber had ever seen. "Ego's 'anonymous' tip-off said we had to solve the *riddle* of Ergo Ego's secret weapon. In legend, the Great Sphinx posed a riddle to those who wished to enter the tomb."

"It's a clue!" declared Amber. "That's where the real McGuffin is!"

"You see?" said Spynosaur with a smirk, "Sometimes the answer is staring you in the face ... and sometimes it's just *lion* there."

Amber was about to groan, but her dad was already racing towards the Sphinx. Amber hurried after him. They darted between the Sphinx's vast feet to a thick stone door beneath the statue's huge chin. Spynosaur sized up the door, before heaving it open with his dino strength.

A luminous-green fog poured out from inside – it was thick and ice-cold and smelled oddly minty.

"What ... what is it?" asked Amber, trying in vain to waft the fog away.

Spynosaur drew his pistol.

"Let's find out, shall we?"

15.
MIND GAMES

 THE SPHINX, CAIRO, EGYPT

"I can't see a thing in all this fog," said Amber, following her dad inside the Sphinx.

"It's a pea-souper all right – it's even messing with my spy-sight," confessed Spynosaur, trying to waft the green smoke away with his tail. "But whatever Ego's hiding in here, I'm sure it's nothing I haven't ... seen ... before..."

Spynosaur ate his words even before they'd left his mouth. The fog suddenly cleared, and he and Amber found themselves not in the gloomy stone innards of the Great Sphinx, but in the middle of a vast, untamed wilderness. They were surrounded by a jungle of verdant vegetation. An endless lake stretched out before them. Thick clouds rolled in a blue sky. In the far distance, a volcano belched plumes of charcoal-black smoke into the air.

"Did – did we take a wrong turn?" gasped Amber, as an impossibly large dragonfly buzzed around her head. "Where are we?"

"Not where ... *when*," replied Spynosaur. He scooped Amber up in his claws and leaped clear as the shadow of a huge grey foot descended upon them, striking the ground with a ground-quaking **THUD**.

Amber looked up. "Dinosaur!" she gasped. A vast *Brachiosaurus* roamed across their path, its every footfall shaking the earth. Behind them, a sail-backed, razor-toothed *Dimetrodon* sized up an armoured, spike-tailed *Ankylosaurus*. In the lake, a huge, finned *Kronosaurus* arched out of the water. And above them, a wide-winged *Pterodactyl* soared, hissing and screeching.

Amber rubbed her eyes. "Did – did we go back in time?" she whispered.

"Don't be fooled, it's just another mind game ... *literally*," replied Spynosaur, glancing around. "The fog we passed through must be some sort of diabolical, brain-bending chemical. We're having a *hallucination*."

"Do you like it? I made it for you!" said a familiar voice.

Spynosaur and Amber spun round. Looming over

the thick jungle, ten times taller than any tree, was
Ergo Ego. He pushed through the forest, trampling
trees and casting his vast shadow over the spies. "I
mean, who doesn't love dinosaurs?"

"You can make us play your games, Ego, but you
can't make us play by your rules," said Spynosaur.
"I'm bringing you in – you and your McGuffin.
And I'm going to do it in time to help Amber with
her homework."

"Da-ad," groaned Amber.

"*And* you'll be no closer to convincing P.O.I.S.O.N. to let you into their criminal club," added Spynosaur with a growl.

"This is not about those stupid heads at P.O.I.S.O.N. letting me join their club!" Ego boomed, shaking the trees. "This is about being the most diabolical villain ever! This is about redefining what it means to be an evil mastermind! This is about proving to those stupid heads at P.O.I.S.O.N. that they should let me join their club!"

Spynosaur and Amber looked at each other and rolled their eyes.

"Wait! I mean... What I meant to say was... Shut up!" boomed Ego. He dabbed his brow with a polka-dot handkerchief and composed himself. "Very soon the forces of villainy will gather for the ultimate demonstration of my super-secret weapon. It's going to be a special day, and I am afraid I simply cannot have you messing it up."

"If it's all the same with you, I prefer to keep death well and truly defied," said Spynosaur, with a flash of sharp teeth.

"You will have to take it up with them!" cackled Ego as he began to fade. Amber and Spynosaur turned ... and saw Ego's illusory dinosaurs pacing towards them.

RRRRRRRRRRR...

"But this is just an illusion, they can't hurt us ... right?" said Amber, edging closer to her father.

"I'm afraid they can," replied her dad. "Ego's brain-fog has created a fully *die-mensional* illusion. Which means if we're killed here ... we die in the real world."

"Great," sighed Amber. Then she struck her most determined ninja stance and roared at the top of her voice. "Come and get it, you dumb dinos! I bet my dad could beat up your dads!"

16.
ATTACK OF THE DINOSAURS

With a cacophony of roars and shrieks, Ergo Ego's army of dinosaurs stormed towards Spynosaur and Amber.

"These perils of prehistory won't stop until we're extinct. Move!" shouted Spynosaur as the armoured *Ankylosaurus* swung its wrecking-ball tail. While Amber threw herself to the ground, Spynosaur launched himself into the air on powerful legs. He landed on the *Ankylosaurus's* back and clung on its rock-hard shell with his claws. The enraged *Ankylosaurus* swung its tail again, just as the *Dimetrodon* lunged. The *Dimetrodon* was struck on the head and fell back, reeling.

"How long until the brain-fog wears off?" asked Amber, skidding underneath a *Diplodocus* tail. "We can't hold them off forev— AAH!"

Suddenly, Amber could see nothing but sky. The *Pterodactyl* had her in its claws.

"Amber! Hang on!" Spynosaur cried, watching the winged . lizard carry his daughter into the air. He dived out of the way of the *Dimetrodon's* snapping jaws, drawing his pistol mid-leap. He aimed and fired before he hit the ground.

" **WHHARK!** " screamed the *Pterodactyl* as the laser seared through its wing.

Amber felt her stomach lurch as the *Pterodactyl* released its grasp on her. She plummeted through the air towards the blue-green waters of the lake.

"AAAAAAAAAA_

POOOOOSH!

"YAAAHahaha!" cried Amber, her scream turning to laughter as she and Spynosaur skyrocketed through the air over the heads of the deadly dinosaurs. Her dad spun in the air, putting himself between Amber and the ground.

THUDD.

"Dad...?" Amber groaned. Her father lay sprawled and winded. Amber's head was spinning as she looked up to see the dinosaurs looming over them. They had her dad in their sights.

"Oi!" shouted Amber. She struggled to her feet, drenched and exhausted ... and struck a pose so battle-ready that she even impressed herself. "If you want my dad, you're going to have to go through me!"

AMBER IS THE SIDEKICK SPY
WHO'LL TAKE ON ANY TASK
IF YOU'RE ON THE HUNT FOR PLUCKINESS
YOU KNOW THE GIRL TO ASK
WITH NINJA MOVES AND SPYING SKILLS
SHE SIMPLY WON'T BE BEATEN
BUT IF THINGS KEEP GOING ON LIKE THIS ...
SHE'S GOING TO GET EATEN

AMBERRRRRRRR!

"SPINNING ELECTRIC OTTER CHOCOLATE BISCUIT WHEELBARROW ATTACK!"

Amber yelled, racing towards the dinosaurs and leaping feet first into the air.

"Amber, wait!" shouted Spynosaur.

As suddenly as they had appeared, the dinosaurs – and their strange prehistoric environment – vanished, to be replaced with the gloomy innards of the stone Sphinx.

Amber found herself flying straight towards a wall.

"Aaaa—"

THUMP.

"As I was trying to tell you, the effects of Ego's brain-fog appear to have worn off," said Spynosaur, getting to his feet.

"Thanks for the – ow – warning," said Amber, lying splayed on the ground. "And now we're back where we started."

"Not quite," said Spynosaur. He glanced around

at the shadowy walls of the Sphinx. Time-bombs lined every surface, each one *tick-tocking* in unison.

"Are those...?" muttered Amber.

"They are indeed," her father replied coolly. He grabbed Amber round the waist and ran towards the entrance faster than she'd ever seen him move. Amber found herself blinded by sunlight as they raced outside and then deafened by an almighty...

Spynosaur and Amber were flung through the air, before skidding and careening across the sand. Spynosaur threw himself on top of Amber as burning rubble rained down across the desert. After a moment they dared to look back – the Sphinx had been blown to smithereens.

"Awesome," Amber said, watching plumes of black smoke billow into the air. "But M11's not going to be happy..."

"She'll forgive us," said Spynosaur. "Because I now know the location of Ego's meeting with P.O.I.S.O.N."

"What? How?" Amber asked.

"It's really very simple — the giant Ergo Ego we encountered in the brain-fog illusion wore a handkerchief covered in polka dots," Spynosaur began. "The polka is the world's eighth silliest dance. 'Dancer' is a reindeer that pulls a sleigh for Father Christmas, also known as Santa Claus. Claws are sharp. B sharp is the third least popular note in music. Music makes the world go round. Round and round we go. 'Go' is the opposite of 'stop'. Stop me if you've heard this one. Two, three, four. Five is the number of times Ergo Ego has tried to kill me. Me, myself and I. Eyes are the windows to the soul. Seoul is the capital of South Korea. A career as a spy can be short-lived. Shorts are worn in summer. Summer follows spring. A spring is a metal coil that can be pressed or pulled but returns to its former shape when released. Release the hounds. Ain't nothing but a hound dog. Dog day afternoon. 'Noon' is another word for midday. Day follows night. Sun follows moon. And, one year ago today, I was tied to a space rocket and fired into the *moon* by Ergo Ego."

"So ... the meeting's on the moon?" suggested Amber.

"So the meeting's in Ego's secret island lair in the Bermuda Triangle!" said Spynosaur. "That's where he'll gather the members of P.O.I.S.O.N. to unveil the real McGuffin. It's so *obvious*. Like he wanted us to know..."

"If you say so," said Amber with a baffled shrug. "But wait a minute — the Department blew up

Ego's lair after he shot you into the moon. It's nothing but smithereens! You can't have a secret meeting in the middle of smithereens."

"He's there, I know it... But I'm still missing something," Spynosaur snarled, tapping his Super Secret Spy Watch™ to activate the Dino-soarer's gravity beam. "Why all the red herrings and wild goose chases? What's the point of it all? I'm starting to wonder if there even is a McGuffin... I'm starting to think we're walking into a trap."

17.
SPYING AND LYING

EN ROUTE TO THE
BERMUDA TRIANGLE

The Dino-soarer had been in the air for almost an hour. Spynosaur had barely said a word since they left Egypt. He hadn't even reported in to M11. He just sat in the pilot's seat, staring out over the sky. Amber had never known him so quiet – he didn't even make any bad puns. It was very unnerving.

I'm starting to think we're walking into a trap.

Amber's ears rang with her father's words. Traps had never seemed to bother her dad in the past... But now it seemed like every time they worked out Ergo Ego's next move, Ego was already one step ahead.

SPYNOSAUR!
COME IN, SPYNOSAUR!

"Dad, it's the Department 6 top-secret transmission channel!" said Amber.

Spynosaur let out a low growl. He narrowed his eyes and pressed a button on the control panel. M11's flustered face appeared on screen.

"M11," Spynosaur said. "It's not a good time."

"Not a good—Blast it to smithereens, Spynosaur, report!" barked M11. "We haven't heard from you since you set off for Cairo. Did you blow up the pyramids? *Please* tell me you didn't blow up the pyramids..."

"Nope! Just the Sphinx!" declared Amber from over her dad's scaly shoulder.

"*Just* the Sphinx? You mean, *just* the immeasurably significant ancient historical monument?" howled M11. "This is why I have a stomach ulcer the size of a baby's fist, Spynosaur! Did you at least secure the McGuffin?"

"Even better!" Amber replied. "We know where Ergo Ego is planning to—"

"Nothing to report, M11," interrupted Spynosaur, jabbing Amber with his tail. "Just more duff McGuffins and dead ends... The trail went cold in Egypt."

Amber immediately replayed that last moment in her head. Her dad had lied to M11. Spies lied to everyone ... *except other spies.* She watched M11's moustache twitch with suspicion.

"I don't need to tell you that if Ego unleashes his super-secret weapon, it's not going to look good on our annual report," M11 said. "We must do whatever it takes to stop him, so if you know something you're not telling me, then you'd jolly well better—"

"You're breaking up, M11," said Spynosaur. With that, he punched the screen with his clawed fist, sending sparks flying across the cockpit. "Bad signal. Call you later."

"Uh, you know there's an 'Off' button just there..." Amber muttered.

Spynosaur activated the autopilot and turned to his daughter.

"Listen to me," he said, placing his claws on Amber's shoulders. "Being a spy is about trusting your instincts. And staying cool under pressure ... and blowing things up ... and being incredibly impressive ... but mostly it's about trusting your instincts. And my instincts tell me that bringing the Department in on this is a mistake. My instincts tell me I have to do this alone."

"Danger Monkey smells funny anyway... OK, fine!" Amber huffed. "We'll do it on our own."

"No, not us," said Spynosaur. "Just me."

"Wait, just you without me? No way!" cried Amber, recoiling. "We're a team! You're the super-secret agent dinosaur and I'm your super-secret-agent-in-training sidekick!"

"But my instincts—" began Spynosaur.

"Your instincts also told you it's a trap!" Amber cried. "And last time you went to the Bermuda Triangle you got shot into the moon! I remember, 'cos I saw it happen! And I don't want you to get shot into the moon again, because I don't want to lose you again!"

"I'm sorry ... but my mind is made up," said Spynosaur firmly.

"But—"

"You're staying put — that's an *order*," added Spynosaur. "Do you understand?"

"Yeah," his daughter replied. "I s'pose."

But Amber Gambit had no intention of doing what she was told.

10.
THE LAIR-WITHIN-A-LAIR

Amber watched Spynosaur race away, his broad, scaly head low, his long tail stretched out behind him. Two minutes earlier they had landed on an island in the middle of the Bermuda Triangle, a short walk from Dr Ego's now-destroyed secret lair. The Dino-soarer had settled, silently and invisibly, on a white-sand beach, which would have been pristine, but for the four large boats moored on the shore and numerous sandy footprints heading inland. Amber's dad was right — demolished lair or not, something was happening on Ergo Ego's island.

Amber stared out of the cockpit. All she could see were palm trees and distant mountains.

Wait here, her dad had told her. *If I'm not back in an hour ... just go.*

Amber waited for a full eighteen seconds before she hurried after Spynosaur.

"I spy with my little eye..." muttered Amber as she scrambled through the bombed-out wreckage of Ergo Ego's old secret lair. It was hard to miss, although nothing but debris remained after Department 6 blew it to smithereens. Amber was careful to move slowly — not just because it looked like the island had visitors, but because she didn't want to get caught by her dad and have her sidekick privileges revoked.

"I spy..." Amber whispered again, following her father's distinctive footprints through a sea of

dust and rubble. Then she spotted something ...
something oddly out of place. In the middle of
the rubble stood a large sign, which read:

SECRET MEETING
OF EVIL
MASTERMINDS
THIS WAY ↓

"*This* way?" said Amber, glancing downwards.
There, embedded in the ground, was a large steel
disc, like a manhole cover, with a red button in its
centre. Amber pressed the button with her foot.

With a **VMM-KLUNK!** the cover dropped open,
revealing a hole plunging into darkness. Amber
peered inside.

There was a ladder.

"Another secret lair underneath the first secret lair... A lair-within-a-lair!" noted an impressed Amber. Then she took a deep breath, pulled up her sleeves and clambered down into the darkness.

The long climb led to a dimly lit corridor, which in turn led to three more corridors. Amber tiptoed towards a distant blue light until she reached a large pair of double doors, open just enough to let the illumination from inside pour out. She edged towards it and heard a familiar voice.

"Welcome to my inner sanctum! Does everyone have what they need? We have an assortment of savoury nibbles, plus those irresistible little tubs of ice cream. Please, make yourselves comfortable..."

"*Ergo Ego...!*" whispered Amber. She peered through the doorway into a large steel-grey room, with high metal gantries stretching round its perimeter. A small army of black clad henchmen lined the walls beneath them. In the centre of the room was a long stone table, round which sat four figures. At the head of the table sat Ergo Ego, shuffling excitedly, the room's bluish light glinting off his egg-shaped head.

"I'm not going to lie, this is a very exciting day for me! P.O.I.S.O.N.'s most vile and villainous, here in my secret island lair-within-a-lair!" said Ego, dabbing his brow nervously. "Fandango Scaramoosh, Shady Lady, Gums Gambino ... your names are synonymous with sin! The greatest criminal masterminds the world has ever known! You have fingers in every pie and thumbs in every bowl of soup..."

Amber peered closer. Her father was right — P.O.I.S.O.N.'s high command was here!

But where was Spynosaur?

"Get to da point, ya mook! Where's the McGuffin?" added the inhumanly broad-shouldered Gums Gambino, his loose lips flapping like a fish out of water.

"What the massively mouthed mobster means," added Shady Lady, her willowy frame shrouded in darkness, "is that we are ready and waiting for the reveal of your super-secret weapon."

"And it had better be good," added Fandango Scaramoosh, his pearl-white suit and silvery quiff of hair shimmering. "This is the twelfth time you've tried to join the Persons of Infamy, Spite and Occasional Notoriousness, Ego. What in the name of my hairdresser's cat makes you think we'll let you join this time?"

"Because this time," Ego replied, "I can defeat your greatest enemy."

The room fell silent. Amber held her breath.

"We have enemies coming out of our ears, Ego,"
said Shady Lady. "Last month my milkman tried to
murder me..."

"Enemies, perhaps," replied Ego. "But none like
Spynosaur."

"Don't even say dat name what you just said!"
growled Gums Gambino, slamming his fist on
the table. "Half my goons are doin' a stretch in
th' Big House 'cos o' dat scaly mook!"

"He's ruined more rackets, prevented more
plots and foiled more felonies than I care to
count," added Shady Lady.

"To put it bluntly," added Fandango Scaramoosh,
"he's a prehistoric pain in the—"

"Exactly!" said Ego. "For the last year, Spynosaur
has been the bane of your existence. Whenever
you are about to do something, oh, I don't know
... *diabolical*, there he is, ready and waiting to
spoil your day." Ego looked up at the gantries high

above them. "Isn't that right ... Spynosaur?"

Amber clamped her hand over her mouth to silence a gasp and looked up. Crouched on one of the gantries, as still and silent as a photograph, was her father.

"I can totally see you up there, you know!" Ego declared. "I mean, you're a dinosaur – you're like the least inconspicuous spy ever." He picked up a bowl of Twiglets from the table. "Come down and join the party! The nibbles are *to die for...*"

Amber saw a flash of movement and sharp teeth as Spynosaur leaped down from the gantry. He landed in the middle of the table and let out a deep, hissing snarl.

"A quintet of criminality," Spynosaur growled. "The game's over for all of you!"

"Over? I'm just getting started! Or rather, you are," said Ego with a grin.

He gestured at the thirty or so henchmen surrounding them. They drew knives, knuckledusters, baseball bats – one even brandished a folding chair. "I know they're not technically my henchmen to command," added Ego, "but if I may be so bold ... get him!"

19.
THE REAL McGUFFIN

With a menacing roar, Spynosaur sprung from the table into the throng of henchmen, a blur of sharp teeth and claws. From her hiding place outside the door, Amber readied herself to dive into the fray, when she remembered what her dad had told her back in the Dino-soarer.

You're staying put – that's an order.

Spynosaur didn't much like giving orders – or following them for that matter – so when he did, Amber knew he meant it.

Besides which, she wasn't sure her dad actually *needed* her help. Spynosaur moved like lightning as he punched, kicked and clawed his way through henchman after henchman, knocking them aside like skittles.

"Hey! what's da big idea, havin' Spynosaur take on our henchmen?" growled Gums Gambino.

"Please, stay in your seats," Ego begged the

P.O.I.S.O.N. high command as another henchman flew across the table. "I promise you, this will all be over soon..."

"After which time Spynosaur will turn his attention to us!" declared Fandango Scaramoosh. "Where's the nearest secret escape route?"

"I assure you, there is no need to panic," said Ego, a henchman whizzing over his head. "Everything is going according to plan."

THERE'S NO ONE QUITE LIKE SPYNOSAUR
A HERO TO US ALL
WE'VE A HUNCH HE'LL BEAT THESE HENCHMEN
AND LEAVE THEM IN A SPRAWL

WHO CAN STOP HIM? NO ONE!
WHAT CAN STOP HIM? NOTHING!
BUT WAIT! THIS IS THE PART WHERE
WE REVEAL THE REAL McGUFFIN...

SPYNOSAUUUUUR!

"Bravo, Spynosaur!" declared Ego, as the last of the henchmen bounced off the table. "Thirty opponents in as many seconds!"

"I'd hate you all to feel left out — let's make it thirty-four, shall we?" Spynosaur said, rounding on Ego and the P.O.I.S.O.N. bigwigs.

"You fool, Ego!" hissed Shady Lady. "You've delivered us straight into Spynosaur's claws!"

"Oh, it's worse than that! If it wasn't for me, there wouldn't even be a Spynosaur!" cackled Ergo Ego. He glared at Spynosaur. "Isn't that right ... Agent Gambit?"

Amber saw her dad bristle.

"So, you know who I am ... or was," said Spynosaur, with a snarl.

"Of course I know, you stupid head!" Ego declared. "I shoot Agent Gambit into the moon, and then you suddenly appear on the scene, with the same fighting style ... the same bad puns ...

the same sidekick, for goodness' sake! It doesn't take a genius to work out that you have Gambit's *brainwaves*. Although yes, I totally am a genius."

"Are you saying that this manicurist's nightmare was once Agent Gambit, the world's greatest secret agent?" gasped Fandango Scaramoosh.

"I can't take credit for the teeth and claws and tail," Ego confessed, wafting his hand in Spynosaur's direction. "You see, I copied Gambit's brainwaves on to one of my patent-pending brain boxes, but it was Department 6 who stole it and used it to transfer the brainwaves of Agent Gambit into this dinosaur. And you can't argue with the results!"

A dozen holographic screens appeared in the air, surrounding Spynosaur and the collected criminals. Spynosaur narrowed his lizard eyes, as Amber peeked her head further round the door to get a better look at the screens. Ego had recorded everything they'd done over the last two days. But why?

"I didn't realize you were such a fan of my work, Ego," said Spynosaur coolly.

"Indeed I am!" laughed Ego. "In fact, over the last forty-eight hours I have tested every aspect of your remarkable abilities to the limit. Your strength, intelligence, speed, endurance ... your courage and skill. And every time, against all the odds, you emerged victorious. Now the esteemed members of P.O.I.S.O.N. know exactly what you are capable of... Now they know the power of my super-secret weapon!"

"The McGuffin? It doesn't exist. It never did," Spynosaur growled. "This whole mission was just red herrings and wild goose chases. But why?"

"You really haven't worked it out, have you?" replied Ego with a sneer. He opened his arms wide and let out a maniacal cackle. "It's you, Spynosaur! You are my super-secret weapon. You are the real McGuffin!"

20.
EGO SAYS, SPYNOSAUR OBEYS

"What are you talking about?" snarled Spynosaur, circling Ego and the malevolent masterminds of P.O.I.S.O.N. "I may be mind-blowingly impressive, but I'm no weapon. You've lost whatever's left of your mind, Ego."

From the doorway, Amber watched her dad growling impatiently, and heard the **CLIK-CLAK** of his toe claws as he loomed over his nemesis.

"Then lock me up, Spynosaur!" said Ego. "I surrender!"

"Surrender?" shrieked Fandango Scaramoosh, glancing incredulously at the members of P.O.I.S.O.N. "Scandalous! A villain never surrenders!"

"They're going to throw away the key on you, Ego," said Spynosaur, squaring up to him. "I'll make sure you never—"

"Ego says stop right there," Ego interrupted.

Spynosaur froze.

"Ego says ... stand on one leg!" added Ego.

Spynosaur duly lifted a clawed foot off the floor.

He stood there, a strangled snarl emanating from his throat. It was as if his body suddenly wouldn't do as it was told. Or rather, his body would only do as it was told by Ergo Ego.

"Dad...?" whispered Amber.

"Ego says, tell me that I am the greatest criminal mastermind ever," Ego said.

Spynosaur seemed to tremble, his eyes wide with rage. Then, through a mouthful of sharp, gritted teeth, he said:

"You ... are the greatest ... criminal mastermind ... ever."

"Yes, I am, you stupid head!" shrieked Ego with glee.

"Dad, no...!" Amber gasped.

"I gotta be seein' things here!" said Gums Gambino, inspecting the frozen Spynosaur.

"How comes this mook is doin' whatever you tells him?"

"Because if Ergo Ego says, Spynosaur obeys!" cackled Ego. "You see, when I mined Agent Gambit's mind, I installed a failsafe – a way to control that mind using only my voice. When I realized his brain box had been used to create Spynosaur, I knew then that I could make Department 6's greatest spy into my greatest weapon!"

Amber clamped both her hands over her mouth. Her dad was right – all this time Ego had been one step ahead of them ... but in a way they couldn't have imagined. She looked back down the corridor. She knew her dad would tell her to go for help if he could. But how could she leave him here, with them? What if she never saw him again?

"Distinguished villains, Spynosaur is the key to your domination of the world! He will crush your enemies ... tear Department 6 apart from the inside – even tie your shoelaces if I command it!

No one will be left to stop you," said Ego. "Or should I say, us?"

The members of P.O.I.S.O.N. looked at each other ... then at the screens ... then at Spynosaur.

"Congratulations on your conscription to our criminal collective!" declared Shady Lady.

"You're a made man, Ego!" boomed Gums Gambino with glee.

"Welcome to P.O.I.S.O.N.!" added Fandango Scaramoosh. "But wait ... beating up our evil henchmen is one thing, but if Spynosaur is to be a true weapon, he will need to obey even the most diabolical command."

"Aha! You want proof that I can force Spynosaur to act like a villain!" said Ego. "Well since you ask, I have just the thing..."

Amber suddenly realized Ergo Ego was staring right at her.

She turned and ran.

"Ego says, bring back that girl," ordered Ego.

Spynosaur snarled and drew his grapple gun. With a **FOOOOOOOOOOOSH!** he launched the grappling hook through the tiny gap in the doorway. It speared Amber's spy-suit at the shoulder and retracted, dragging her back up the corridor and through the doorway. Before she knew it, Amber found herself in the middle of the room, being glared at by four criminal masterminds ... and her own father.

"What have you done to my dad, you baldy stinker?" Amber snarled, struggling to detach herself from the grappling hook.

"Well, you are no more charming than the last time we met," said Ego. "Members of P.O.I.S.O.N., here is the final proof of my pudding – Spynosaur's own sidekick, who, by the way, is also his daughter!"

"Dad...?" Amber said, looking up at her father. He stared back, helpless to do anything but obey his new master.

"There's a good little slave," Ego sneered, patting Spynosaur on the shoulder. "But wait, you haven't touched the nibbles – Ego says you must be hungry."

 growled Spynosaur.

"I thought so... So eat her," said Ergo Ego. "Ego says, eat your daughter!"

21.
AMBER VS SPYNOSAUR

"My dad's not going to eat me!" Amber protested, freeing herself from the grappling hook and leaping to her feet. Spynosaur loomed over her, claws and teeth bared. "Right, Dad...?"

"Silly sidekick, there is no 'Dad'!" screamed Ergo Ego. "There is only Spynosaur, my slave!"

Spynosaur roared in Amber's face, his hot breath stinging her eyes. Then he reared back ... and struck. **"LAST–MINUTE CHEWING GUM SPLIT–SECOND LIMBO MANOEUVRE!"** Amber cried, leaning backwards until her head nearly touched the floor.

Spynosaur's jaws clamped shut inches from her face with a **SNAPP!**

"**SCRAMBLED EGG WHIRLWIND WET~TOWEL DEVASTATING HUMMINGBIRD ATTACK!**" Amber yelled. She dropped on to her hands and spun her legs in the air, landing both feet hard on the side of her dad's head.

"**RR...AAAAGH!**"

screamed an enraged Spynosaur. Amber saw a blur of movement as her dad's huge tail rushed towards her. Her last thought as she was knocked unconscious was of her dad – not as he was now, but as he was a year ago, on that fateful day when everything changed...

Let my dad go, you baldy-headed stinker!

I might as well ... I have all I need from your father – namely, his brainwaves!

Thanks to my mind-mining machine, everything that makes Agent Gambit the world's greatest secret agent is stored here, in this brain box. I'm afraid Daddy dearest has outlived his usefulness!

Amber, get that brain box ... and then get out of here! I love you, Amber!

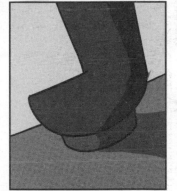

Dad! DAAAD!

"Dad!"

Amber woke with a start and looked around. She was in Ergo Ego's inner sanctum. Spynosaur's blow had sent her skidding under the stone table. She winced silently as she tried to move. Then she heard the **CLIK-CLAK** of her father's toe-claws tapping on the ground. He snorted loudly, sniffing the air. She saw his shadow on the ground. A moment later a claw grabbed the edge of the table and flung it into the air.

"RRRR..." growled Spynosaur, head low and jaws snapping. Only his eyes betrayed his desperation.

"Snap out of it! Come back to me, Dad!" Amber pleaded, trying to drag herself across the floor.

But Spynosaur stopped her in her tracks by pressing a great clawed foot on her back. "I lost you once when you got shot into the moon! I don't want to lose you again... Please, come back!"

"Enough! Ego says, finish her!" Ergo Ego ordered.

Amber closed her eyes. Then, as her dad's jaws opened, his razor-sharp teeth glinting, Amber had an idea. It was such a horrible idea that she immediately tried to banish it from her head.

"Please don't make me do it," she whispered to herself. "Please don't make me do it, please don't make me do it, please don't make me do it..."

But she knew she had no choice. She had one chance to save herself. One chance to save her father...

...And it would be the most embarrassing thing EVER.

22.
SPYNOSAUR'S SECRET WEAPON

"I'm a little teapot, short and stout," Amber sang softly, her cheeks reddening.

"Here's my handle, here's my spout..."

"What ... what's she doing?" snapped Ergo Ego.

"Are – are you singing?"

Amber's face flushed red with humiliation.

"When I get all steamed up, hear me shout," she sang through gritted teeth.

"Tip me up and pour me out..."

"*RRRR...*" Spynosaur growled.

"What larks!" noted Fandango Scaramoosh.

"A doomed sidekick, humiliating herself further

for no apparent reason! It's these sort of moments a villain lives for..."

"I'm a little teapot, short and stout!" Amber sang, quicker this time. "Here's my handle, here's my spout. When I get all steamed up, hear me shout, tip me up and pour me out!"

"RRRRR..."

"I'm a little teapot, short and stout. Here's my handle, here's my spout. when I get all steamed up, hear me——"

"Enough!" said Ego, striding over to Spynosaur. "What're you waiting for, slave? Ego says, eat her!"

Spynosaur let out a low growl. Then he turned to face Ergo Ego.

"Ego," Spynosaur said, "you must be out of your mind."

"Wh-what?" blurted Ergo Ego. "Ego says, I didn't say you could speak! How did you——?"

"Didn't you work it out, Ego? I've got a super-secret weapon, too," replied Spynosaur, helping his daughter to her feet. "Her name is Amber."

WHOMP.

With a flick of Spynosaur's tail, Ergo Ego flew across the room, bouncing and skidding until he landed with a **FUDD!** on top of the pile of P.O.I.S.O.N.'s henchmen.

"I appear to be back," said Spynosaur, ruffling Amber's hair with a claw. "What would I do without my poppet?"

"Da-ad, not in front of the evil masterminds..." Amber groaned, still red with embarrassment.

The members of P.O.I.S.O.N. turned tail and raced towards the doorway.

Without warning, the wall of Ego's inner sanctum blew open, and twenty armed-to-the-teeth Department 6 agents rushed in, surrounding the panicked villains.

"Ain't nobody going nowhere!" came a cry as Danger Monkey, his tail fixed in plaster, strode triumphantly inside. "Move a muscle an' I'll gnaw your eyebrows! I'll spit in your dinner! I'll post unflatterin' remarks about you on social media!"

A moment later, M11 strode through the assemblage of agents, her moustache twitching victoriously. "Well, well ... the world's most unspeakable rotters, all together in one room," she said, glaring at the cowed criminals. "I don't suppose I have to tell you that under Amendment Thirteen-point-two of Article 6 of the Anti-Infamy Imperative, you are duly retained at the pleasure of Her Majesty the Queen of so on and so forth."

"In other words, yer *nicked*," Danger Monkey added.

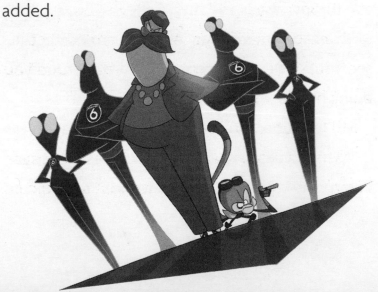

"It's a stitch-up!" cried Gums Gambino.

"What a drag..." sighed Fandango Scaramoosh.

"We're cornered and collared!" wailed Shady Lady. "Ego, consider your consideration for membership ... unconsidered!"

"Wait ... don't go..." groaned Ego from the pile of henchmen. "I have more nibbles..."

It wasn't long before Danger Monkey and the agents were leading the lair-full of lawbreakers (masterminds or otherwise) back up to the surface as M11, Spynosaur and Amber looked on.

"Don't get me wrong, M11, it's always nice to see you," Spynosaur remarked. "But what are you doing here?"

M11 let out an exasperated tut.

"As hard as you may find it to believe, Spynosaur, I didn't get where I am today without a modicum of common sense – I had a hunch you were on to something, so I had Dr Newfangle track the Dino-soarer here." She looked round. "I assume you found the McGuffin?"

"Well, to be honest—" Spynosaur began.

"There never was a McGuffin," Amber quickly interrupted. "It was all just wild herrings and red goose chases! And *definitely* no singing."

"I see. Well, in that case it's a job well done," M11 concluded happily. "And you didn't even blow anything to smithereens!"

Spynosaur glanced at Amber, and grinned.

"The day's not over yet," he said.

23.
BUSINESS IS BOOMING

Ten minutes later, Spynosaur and Amber were taking to the air aboard the Dino-soarer. They sat in the cockpit, hovering above Ergo Ego's secret island lair-within-a-lair as the last of Department 6's helicopters headed for the horizon.

"Dad, I know you're probably never going to forgive me for disobeying you," said Amber. "But I am never *ever* going to forgive you for making me sing that song in public."

"Well, it certainly struck just the right *note* with me," replied her dad. "It was quick thinking, using that tune to free me from Ego's control."

"I s'pose ... just don't make me do it again. *Ever,*"

Amber huffed. Then she leaned over and gave her dad a hug. "So now what? Ergo Ego and the whole of P.O.I.S.O.N., all locked up. What are we going to do?"

"Oh, I'm not sure we'll be out of a job any time soon. If you're a spy trying to save the world from villainy, business is booming." Spynosaur looked out of the cockpit window, and stroked his chin with a deadly claw. "But, I can't help thinking something's still not quite right..."

"What is it? Do you think we missed something?" asked Amber. "Do you think Ergo Ego has got another trick up his sleeve?"

"No ... I just noticed his lair-within-a-lair is not

in the least blown up," added her dad, aiming the Dino-soarer's missile launchers at the island. "Would you care to do the honours, pop— Amber?"

"Me? Really?" squealed Amber excitedly.

"Well, you *did* save the world," said Spynosaur. He flipped open the cover on the button labelled "BOOM" and gave Amber a wink. "And didn't I tell you the spy business was *booming*?"

Amber let that one go. She just grinned and pressed the button.

HE'S THE SPY THAT SURPRISES!
HE'S THE AGENT WHO'LL AMAZE!

BEATING ODDS AND VILLAINY
AND SAVING ALL THE DAYS!

EGO WOULD HAVE USED HIM AS

A SUPER-SECRET WEAPON

BUT AMBER SANG A TEAPOT SONG
WHICH MEANT THAT DIDN'T HAPPEN!

SPYNOSAUR!

SO IF YOU NEED A HERO WHO'S A CUT ABOVE THE REST

THEN DO WHAT ERGO EGO DID AND PUT HIM TO THE TEST

AMBER AND HER FATHER ARE ON HAND TO SAVE THE DAY

AND BLOW STUFF UP TO SMITHEREENS
IF IT GETS IN THEIR WAY!

SPYNOSAUR!
SPYNOSAUUUUUR!

EPILOGUE

LITTLE WALLOP PRIMARY SCHOOL,
LITTLE WALLOP, ENGLAND,
THE UNITED KINGDOM OF GREAT
BRITAIN AND NORTHERN IRELAND,
EARTH

Amber's mum was waiting outside the gates of Little Wallop Primary School in time to see Amber and her friends head out of the gates.

"See you tomorrow!" Amber's friends called after her.

The disguised Sergei gave a disgruntled wave, before Amber's mum gave him a hug.

"So, did you have a good day?" she asked as they made their way home. "How did you do on your test?"

"I passed, of course. My score was total of one hundred per cent," replied Sergei. "It should not be surprise. In my country I was top of classes at Spy Academy."

There was a long silence, as Amber's mum stared at Sergei. After a moment she chuckled and put her hand on Sergei's shoulder.

"Amber Gambit," she said with a smile. "You have *such* an imagination."

DEPARTMENT

6

CLASSIFILES

CODE NAME:
SPYNOSAUR

AKA:
Agent Gambit, A47

Primary Spy-ciality:
Advanced Spying

Secondary Spy-ciality:
Puns

Motto:
"I'm going to make
crime extinct."

With the brainwaves
of top super-spy Agent
Gambit and the body
of a Deinonychus,
Spynosaur is the
world's only Super
Secret Agent Dinosaur!
Specializes in
stylishly saving the
world, defying death
and infuriating his
boss, M11. Spynosaur is
an expert combatant, a
cunning detective and a
master of disguise ...
as long as no one spots
his tail.

DEPARTMENT
6

CODE NAME:
AMBER

AKA: Amber Gambit,
"Dad's Little Poppet"

Primary Spy-ciality:
Ninja stuff

Secondary Spy-ciality:
Spy stuff

Motto:

"THUNDEROUS LEAPING
BAGUETTE FIVE OCELOTS
ATTACK!"

Spynosaur's daughter
and sidekick, Amber
Gambit is as dedicated
as her dad to fighting
crime and foiling
fiends wherever they
find them. Highly
resourceful and
skilled, with more
ninja moves than you
can shake a foot at,
Amber Gambit keeps her
double life and ninja
skills secret - even
from her mum.

DEPARTMENT
6

CODE NAME:
DANGER MONKEY

AKA: A41

Primary Spy-ciality:
Espionage

Secondary Spy-ciality:
Monkey business

Motto:

"I'll eat yer chips!"
"I'll brush yer hair
the wrong way!"

"I'll write a haiku
mockin' yer personal
hygiene!"

A foul-mouthed,
banana-chomping
spider monkey.
Skillful but small;
weakness for fruit;
tendency to fling his
own poo. Agent A41's
mind was transferred
into the body of a
spider monkey using
"brain box" technology
retro-engineered
by Dr Newfangle.

DEPARTMENT
6

CLASSIFILE

CODE NAME:
GUMS GAMBINO

Motto:

"What's da big idea, havin' da big idea to have a big idea?"

Founding member of P.O.I.S.O.N. (PERSONS OF INFAMY, SPITE & OCCASIONAL NOTORIOUSNESS), crime boss Gums Gambino grew up on the mean streets and the unkind lanes, to become the most ruthless gangster ever to put on a pin-stripe suit. Gambino is thoroughly hard-bitten, which is ironic because he lost all his teeth in a power-cut during a routine dental check-up.

DEPARTMENT
6

CODE NAME:
FANDANGO SCARAMOOSH

Motto:

"I've got miles of style and time for crime!"

Founder Member of P.O.I.S.O.N. (PERSONS OF INFAMY, SPITE & OCCASIONAL NOTORIOUSNESS), Fandango Scaramoosh may have been a poor boy from a poor family, but his ambition was as large as his ego, which was as large as his enormous silvery quiff of hair. The flamboyant felon quickly rose through the criminal ranks to become the world's most manicured mastermind. Scaramoosh cares almost as much about looking fabulous as he does about taking over the world.

CODE NAME:
SHADY LADY

Motto:

"No lady is
more shady."

Charter member
of P.O.I.S.O.N.
(PERSONS OF INFAMY,
SPITE & OCCASIONAL
NOTORIOUSNESS) The
shadowy figure
known only as
Shady Lady is
constantly shrouded
in darkness and
mystery. Deceptive,
deceitful, devilish
and diabolical,
Shady Lady will
stab you in the
back while kissing
you on the cheek.
And steal your
wallet for good
measure.

DEPARTMENT
6

CODE NAME:
AGENT GAMBIT
〖REDACTED〗

〖REDACTED〗

DEPARTMENT
6

CODE NAME:
MRS GAMBIT

Amber's mum.

DON'T TELL HER
ANYTHING.

DEPARTMENT
6